Magpie Gabbard
and the Quest
for the Buried Moon

Magpie Gabbard

and the Quest for the Buried Moon

Sally M. Keehn

PHILOMEL BOOKS

Patricia Lee Gauch, Editor

PHILOMEL BOOKS
A division of Penguin Young Readers Group.
Published by The Penguin Group.
Penguin Group (USA) Inc., 375 Hudson Street, New York, NY 10014, U.S.A.
Penguin Group (Canada), 90 Eglinton Avenue East, Suite 700, Toronto, Ontario, Canada
M4P 2Y3 (a division of Pearson Penguin Canada Inc.).
Penguin Books Ltd, 80 Strand, London WC2R 0RL, England.
Penguin Ireland, 25 St. Stephen's Green, Dublin 2, Ireland (a division of Penguin Books Ltd.).
Penguin Group (Australia), 250 Camberwell Road, Camberwell, Victoria 3124, Australia
(a division of Pearson Australia Group Pty Ltd).
Penguin Books India Pvt Ltd, 11 Community Centre, Panchsheel Park,
New Delhi—110 017, India.
Penguin Group (NZ), Cnr Airborne and Rosedale Roads, Albany, Auckland 1310,
New Zealand (a division of Pearson New Zealand Ltd).
Penguin Books (South Africa) (Pty) Ltd, 24 Sturdee Avenue,
Rosebank, Johannesburg 2196, South Africa.
Penguin Books Ltd, Registered Offices: 80 Strand, London WC2R 0RL, England.

Design by Semadar Megged.   Text set in 12.5 point Aldus.

Library of Congress Cataloging-in-Publication Data
Keehn, Sally M.
Magpie Gabbard and the quest for the buried moon / Sally M. Keehn.   p. cm.
Summary: In Kentucky in 1872, when goblins capture the moon, thirteen-year-old Magpie
must rise above her family's fighting legacy and put her "cussedness" to use to save the
moon and her loved ones, according to "the age-old prophecy."
[1. Family life—Kentucky—Fiction. 2. Vendetta—Fiction. 3. Moon—Fiction. 4. Goblins—Fiction.
5. Kentucky—History—1865—Fiction. 6. Tall tales.] I. Title.
PZ7.K2257Mag 2007   [Fic]—dc22   2006008920
ISBN 978-0-399-24340-0
1 3 5 7 9 10 8 6 4 2
First Impression

This one's for Molly—
who keeps us focused on the sunny side.

Chapter One

The Letter

Gabbard Mountain, Kentucky
October 2, 1872

Dear All and Sundry,
I mean to visit my brother Milo and give him back his
foot. YOU KNOW HOW MUCH HE NEEDS THAT FOOT. No
one's gonna stop me. I'm thirteen. Now don't fret
about my going off-mountain where I ain't never
been. And with a dark night coming on. I know them
Goblins will be on the rise—ever ready to sink their
teeth into my tender neck. And yes, there'll be vicious
Sizemores further on down the road just itching to
plug me with a bullet to the brain. But I'll be all right.
It's my thirteenth birthday. I've got magic sparkles
coming to me. I've also got me a plan for getting
to Milo.
You've always told me, "It's good to have a plan."
Love to all of you but Randall,
Magpie

1

Chapter Two
The Plan

Milo's got a remarkable foot. It ain't turned gray and withered the way you'd think a chopped-off foot would do. It looks natural—complete to the dirt between the toes. I've now got it cushioned between two corn bread slabs and hidden in my apron pocket. Thank goodness Big Mama made that pocket extra wide! She knows I like to carry things along with me. Once I carried a picnic in this pocket. Just last May. At that time, Milo still had both his feet. He'd wanted to have a picnic to celebrate the blooming of our dogwood, but the coughing sickness had come over Milo—making him too weak to walk.

So Randall (he's my other brother—now turned mean enough to skin a cat alive) carried Milo on down to our favorite spot—the Everlasting Spring. There, the three of us joked and ate corn bread, cheese and dried apples. We listened to bullfrogs croak.

That was the last picnic us three had.

A vase filled with wildflowers now covers the spot where Milo's foot once stood on our fireplace mantelpiece. Big Mama mustn't discover that foot's gone from there until I'm safely OUT OF HERE. She believes that foot's her guarantee that one day Milo will return to claim it. And then, she'll lock him up and make him stay with us forever because she loves him—as do we all.

Even if Milo wanted to, I can't see how he could return. It's one thing to hop down our steep mountain slope on your one remaining foot. It's another to hop back up. It'd take all the breath you had and Milo never had much to begin with. He's been sickly since birth. Him, so pale and white, like one of them beautiful marble angels I once seen in my Grandpa Gabbard's *European Art and Architecture* book.

But as sickly as Milo's always been, I've never heard him fret about it. He's too full of music to fret. He makes the finest trumpet music you ever heard. He don't do it by blowing on a trumpet horn—like you might think. He does it by squeezing air between his hands. The music he makes with his hands can make you laugh. It can make you cry. It can prime you to take on anything—including your own Big Mama.

I hear her now—banging around in the kitchen where she's boiling up water for my thirteenth birthday bath. I sneak in behind her and grab up my Grandpa Gabbard's saw-toothed knife—used for cutting off honeycombs. I grab a bucket. Big Mama, at the sink, turns and hollers at me, "Two cups of honey, Magpie! I need two cups. One for your bath. The other for your cake. I'm making a big one. Them Goforths are coming to celebrate your birthday. There'll be thirteen mouths to feed."

"I hear you, Big Mama." With knife and bucket in hand, I hurry for the cabin door. Big Mama's got her reasons for the getting of honey. I got mine. Wait 'til you see what I plan to lure out of the brush with a bucket of honey! If I get my timing right, I'll mount that something. It'll carry me down-mountain and over to Milo in less than a day.

I'll hand him his foot.

We'll talk the way we used to—heart-to-heart.

Milo will put his foot back on. Then he'll move on to where he's dying to go. I won't see him again in my lifetime. It'll grieve my heart—watching him leave.

Still, I'll know I've made him happy—this one last time.

But Big Mama can't catch wind of this. If she knew I was meaning to leave our mountain—and with Milo's foot—she'd chain me up. She'd put me down the Hidey-Hole beneath our cabin floor. I'd never see daylight again nor Milo.

I miss that Milo.

With him gone, I'm nothing but a hollowed-out gourd.

Randall

Elbowing open the cabin door, I step outside onto a spot of sunlight on our porch. I look around for fog. Our mountaintop's a gathering place for fog—particularly in October. I don't see no fog whatsoever—not even in the dip between the outhouse and my Sweet Daddy's work shed.

Glory be, I've got full sunlight on my thirteenth birthday! This must be a surefire sign that magic's in the air. I test the presence of that magic by doing a *heel-toe, heel-toe, shuffle my feet then off I go* and miss my timing. I stumble on a porch step and land on my bottom in the yard.

I reckon the magic of my turning thirteen hasn't stirred the air just yet. When it does, I won't be stumbling over nothing—I hope! I make sure Milo's foot's still in its place in my apron pocket and comfortable between them corn bread slabs.

It is.

I pick myself up and make my way through our flock of chickens, pecking around the sunlit dirt in search of mealy bugs. Big Mama's prized hen, Mehetabel, clucks good morning to me in that special way she has—*cluckty-cluckty.*

"Howdy, Mehetabel." I give her a morning scratch on the neck and then I hurry onward. As I do, my brother Randall steps out from the dark shadow of our woodshed. Randall's the last person on earth I want to see. I thought he'd gone out earlier with Sweet Daddy to bring in the hogs and here Randall is—wood-splitting axe in hand.

He steps right in my way and says, "Where do you think you're going, Skunk?"

I hate the name Skunk. He calls me it on account of the white streak I got running through my night-dark hair.

I tell Randall, "My name's Magpie and where I'm going is none of your business." He knows I'm off to get honey. Why else would I carry this special knife and bucket?

But he don't know of my plan for getting to Milo.

He'd stop me for sure. He's Big Mama's RIGHT-HAND MAN. Randall does everything he thinks Big Mama would want and more.

I sidestep him and he grabs hold of my arm. Randall's got strong hands I can't pull away from no matter how hard I might try. So I don't. I just stand there, staring up at his ugliness.

Randall says, "Everything's my business."

"Do you know you got hairs poking out of that there nose of yours? When you talk *business*, them hairs wave back and forth like they was making fun of you." I know full well that Randall's sensitive about them nose hairs, but I don't care. Ever since Milo left us, I've done all I can to make life miserable for Randall. And Randall—since Milo left—has made life miserable for me.

Chapter Four

Horny Heads

andall's squeezing my arm tight hard, but I don't let on how much it hurts me, because that's what he's looking for and there ain't no way I'm gonna pleasure him. I say to Randall, "If I was you, I'd clip off them nose hairs before you go off courting our cousin Thelma. Seeing them hairs is liable to make her throw up on you. And here she's frying you up some Horny Heads for your noon meal."

Horny Heads are a sucker-type fish that grows little horns on its head. Randall's the only one on this mountaintop who likes to eat them.

"How do you know about them Horny Heads Thelma's cooking up for me?" Randall squeezes my arm ever tighter.

I clench my bucket handle to even out the pain and I say, "I saw Thelma yesterday afternoon and she told me." I don't tell Randall that I found Thelma some Bug Dirt to sprinkle on them fish. Eating Bug Dirt will cause Randall's hair to stick straight out. He'll burp for hours. Them burps will stink like dead rats in the sun. I should know. Sweet Daddy's dogs got hold of Bug Dirt last year and this selfsame thing happened to them.

But I didn't tell Thelma that.

I told her, "This here Bug Dirt's enchanted. When eaten by Randall, it'll turn him sweet."

Thelma believed me. She most always does.

Now, I made a real point of telling Thelma, who likes to overseason things, to only use a pinch of Bug Dirt on each fish. I may want Randall to look like a fool in Thelma's eyes, but I don't want him sick to death. After all, he is my other brother.

And he used to be nice.

Thelma said, "All right, Magpie."

Randall now says, "If you've poisoned Thelma's thoughts against me, I'll hack your heart out." He raises his axe like he might do just that.

I stick out my chest. "Go on! Cut out my heart! What good's my heart now Milo's gone?"

Soon as I say *Milo*, Randall lowers his axe. His face turns white, like I'd thrust a knife blade deep into his heart, causing a hole in it through which all his blood's now draining out. A thought hits me like a bullet to the brain—Randall needs to see Milo and give him back his foot as much as I do.

I can't let Randall come along with me and Milo's foot, safe here in my apron pocket. That ain't part of my plan. Randall needs to stay put and take care of the family. Where would our family be with two sons gone and the one and only daughter, too? We'd be up a creek without a paddle! So I let fly with my bucket. I slam that bucket into Randall's leg. Shrieking in pain, he lets go of me. I race away from him—past the barn and Big Mama's grazing sheep. I duck around the schoolhouse where my Grandpa Gabbard once taught us everything he thought we needed to know in life, including such high-blown words as *pernicious*.

"Watch out for them *pernicious* Sizemores," Grandpa Gabbard liked to say. He hated them Sizemores—a large family of no-accounts living down-mountain in Squabble Town. Even though I have yet to meet a Sizemore face-to-face, I hate them, too. I've heard enough about them to know they're not only *pernicious*, but downright *despicable*.

I head into the sunlit woods. A cold wind blows ripe apple-scented air into my face. It won't be long before winter. It'll be a lonely winter without Milo and his music. But God has called my brother and so he's bound to leave us. There's no fighting that, although I will admit that for a time I tried.

Knife in one hand and bucket in the other, I plunge through a laurel thicket. I startle a covey of quail. They fly upward with a whoosh toward a coverlet of golden leaves. I leap over a pile of windfall like . . . why, like I was a graceful deer. I ain't tripping over my feet. I ain't huffing nor puffing neither. I reckon the magic of turning thirteen is starting to work.

Chapter Five

The Thirteenth Birthday

According to my Big Mama, a girl's thirteenth birthday's real important, for it's the gate between her being a mere child and a woman. Big Mama says if a girl enters this gate with a longing to create a happier world for her family, she'll stir the air, bringing forth the magic sparkles promised her since birth. She only has the one day to call out these sparkles to do her will, so she'd be smart to make the most of their magic in what time she has.

Big Mama told me that the day she turned thirteen, she used her sparkles for a clarifying honey bath. Now a honey bath, in and of itself, softens your skin and turns it the color of a ripe peach. But a *clarifying* honey bath—in which a girl calls on her sparkles to *clarify* her skin—sucks out her pimple-spots, every one.

Big Mama's clarifying bath sucked her skin clean. It turned that skin so soft and beautiful, she drew on the boys. One of them boys fell in love with Big Mama. He courted her for three years and then, he married her.

That loving man is my Sweet Daddy.

Big Mama wants me to have a clarifying honey bath on this, *my* thirteenth birthday. That's why she's boiling up bathwater. That's why she wants that extra cup of honey. Well, I got something more important in mind than clarifying my skin so that I can attract a boy. I got Milo's foot in mind. I need to return it to him in two weeks—by October 16th—that's Milo's deadline, given him by God. The returning of this foot won't be easy nor will it make all members of my family happy.

But it must be done.

Chapter Six

The Moon

As I approach the apple orchard where I mean to put my plan to see Milo into action, I spy the moon. A shining sickle of a moon smiles down at me from the blue October sky. Look at that moon. She's got herself all gussied up. She's turned herself all gold like honey. I've never seen her colored gold. Is she doing this to wish me happy birthday and good luck on my journey to Milo?

I bet she is.

I love the moon.

She named me.

Thirteen years ago to this very day, the moon came all the way to earth to name me. Now, it wasn't as easy as you might think because my Grandpa

Gabbard had already picked out my name. Soon as Grandpa saw me with my black and white hair, he said, "This girl-child with that hair is the spitting image of her Great-Grandmother Margaret who spat in the face of the King of England and got deported here to America because of it!

"I name this girl-child Margaret!"

I'm told I spat in Grandpa's face and Grandpa laughed and said, "Margaret Gabbard, I like your fighting spirit. On account of it, I'm passing on to you my legacy—that being a righteous ire and downright indignation against them lying, cheating, cattle-killing Sizemores. Along with it, I pass on to you a cussedness to carry on the fight with them forever."

If I'd had my birth certificate drawn up on the spot, it would have simply read:

MARGARET GABBARD
Sex FEMALE.
Born OCTOBER 2, 1859
On GABBARD MOUNTAIN, KENTUCKY
AND NOT IN SQUABBLE TOWN WITH ITS
PERNICIOUS SIZEMORES,
·WHICH MARGARET WILL TAKE CARE OF
IN HER OWN GOOD TIME.

However, it just so happened that while Grandpa was passing on a name and a legacy to me *inside* our cabin, Sweet Daddy had taken himself *outside* to have a quiet drink over by his work shed. And who should come to my Sweet Daddy but the moon herself—hidden within her long black cloak.

The moon—who, Sweet Daddy says, watches over all us Gabbard Mountain folk because she loves us dearly—whispered into my Sweet Daddy's ear, "Name the baby Magpie. A magpie's a beautiful black and white bird."

"My baby must be someone real special for you to come to me and with such a high-flying name for her," Sweet Daddy said to the moon.

And the moon replied, "If Magpie can rise above her grandpa's fighting legacy and put her cussedness to good use, one day she could save us all."

"By us all, do you mean you, too?" Sweet Daddy said.

"Me, too," the moon whispered and then, she was gone and the next time Sweet Daddy saw her, she was back up in the sky.

And so on the night of my birth, I was given two names, a legacy and a prophecy. Now, I can handle two first names. And I reckon I can carry on my grandpa's legacy. I've got enough cussedness in me to fight them Sizemores into eternity.

It's the prophecy that puzzles me.

How am I to save us all? And what am I to save us from? And when? I wish Sweet Daddy had stopped the moon from leaving so that she could tell him. But he didn't. And so we're left with questions too big for us to answer, although we've tried.

Sweet Daddy and I have agreed on one thing. Nothing bad will ever happen to the moon. Even those Goblins down in Cob Hollow who'd like to kill her off so's they could take over the night forever and eat up everything alive are no match for her.

She's too big and bright and powerful.

Chapter Seven

Wild Bill

Nineteen years ago, when Grandpa Gabbard brought our clan out of Squabble Town and up here to this mountaintop, he brought his bees with him. He hollowed out a bee gum to house their hive and placed it in the middle of his apple orchard. Here his bees proceeded to make their remarkable honey. Humans crave that honey. Not only is it helpful in baths, but eating it turns teeth white as snow, besides which, the honey tastes real good.

Wild creatures crave that honey, too.

Most wild creatures rob the bee gum on the quiet, when we ain't looking. But there's one—the wiliest, the most dangerous creature of all—who likes us humans to do the robbing for him. Once we've got our bucket of honey, he charges us from behind, knocks us teacup over kettle and takes it all for himself.

He's been doing this for years.

It's that creature who could carry me to Milo.

If I get my timing right.

As I slowly approach Grandpa's bee gum, I hear just what I expected—a soft *hee-hawg*. It comes from the bramble patch off to my left where I know the creature likes to make his nest.

I pretend that I don't hear him.

Acting like this was just another day, I draw near the bee gum. Slowly, carefully, for I happen to know Grandpa's bees don't like sudden moves or noises, I tilt up the wooden lid. No bees come buzzing out at me. I reckon them bees are real drowsy, what with the bite of winter in the air.

I hitch the bucket handle over the crook of my left arm so I have both hands free. I circle my head to clear my brain. I whisper, "Magic birthday sparkles, come on out and help me now, I pray." Wonder of wonders, tiny sparks of light instantly hum through the air around me—*my sparkles*. I breathe them in. Sparkles fizzle up my nose and into my brain. They make me feel strong, powerful and sure of myself.

With my knife, I cut off a comb of honey that's

stuck to the bee gum's lid. I ease the knife along with the comb into my bucket. I close the lid and I let out with a loud and satisfying "Ahhhhhhh."

I back away from the bee gum—one step, two step, three. I breathe in more sparkles. I feel as ready as I'll ever be. I now do something I know the creature in the bramble patch can't resist. I turn my back on him and walk away.

He grunts. He always grunts before he attacks.

When I hear the sound of his thundering hooves, I stop. I bend my knees. *It's now or never.* I shift my weight onto my tiptoes. The giant creature catches me in the bottom with his snout and I spring. I arch through the air and curl into a backward somersault. I land, seated, on the creature's back.

My honey bucket dangles from my arm. I still have Milo's foot in my apron pocket. I'm set. I've done it. With the help of my sparkles and Grandpa's honey I've just mounted the most vicious boar you ever saw—Wild Bill. He's also the fastest. He once carried Claire Sizemore (a girl whose last name I spit on every time I say it) from Squabble Town to New York City—all in one day.

I grab hold of Wild Bill's ears and I shout into them: "Wild Bill! Take me to my brother Milo!"

And the giant boar sinks beneath me.

Now I ain't never ridden a wild boar. And when I've tried to ride Sweet Daddy's mule, she's always thrown me. But I'm thirteen. My sparkles hum. I do what now comes natural-like—I sink along with Wild Bill. My feet hit the ground. He sinks even lower. I sink, too.

This boar's readying himself for the takeoff.

"Wild Bill! Take me to Milo!" I scream.

The boar explodes beneath me. He bucks. He kicks. He's trying to get rid of me! I call on my sparkles. With their help, I stick like glue to Wild Bill's back even though he now bucks so hard it hurts my bones.

"You listen here! You'd better take me to Milo or else!" I bang my legs against Wild Bill's bucking sides. The old boar comes down on all fours and then he bolts with me. I clench his ears as he charges with me through rows of apple trees. The bucket of honey bangs against Wild Bill's neck, which sets him into squealing fit to die.

"Take me to Milo! Take me to Milo!" I scream.

Wild Bill scrambles down the stony outcrop at the back of our outhouse. I hang on for all I'm worth. He carries me past Big Mama's bleating sheep, Sweet Daddy's woodshed, the hay rake, the barn and toward the trail that passes by my cabin before turning sharply right at Dead Man's Cliff to head down-mountain.

Wild Bill gallops faster and faster. Soon, no doubt, he'll lift off the ground. He'll fly me to my brother. I can hardly wait. I keep screaming, "Take me to Milo," so Wild Bill won't forget where we need to go.

And just when I think I'm set, that in moments I'll be handing Milo's foot to him, a dark figure carrying a shotgun limps out from my cabin—just ahead. It's Randall. Big Mama comes out right behind him. She shrieks, "Magpie! Where do you think you're going? You'll get yourself killed!

"Randall! Stop your sister! Stop her now!"

Randall's shotgun blast shatters the air above Wild Bill and me. The boar turns to flee in one direction. I head straight on in the other. I don't even have time to call on my sparkles for help. I fly over Wild Bill's head. I catch the golden glimmer of the setting moon. Then I tuck my head and roll, doing a half a somer-sault, before smacking the earth with the small of my back.

Chapter Eight

Cussedness

I now float facedown in a bath of warm honey-laced water Big Mama has prepared for me even though I told her, "I ain't got sparkles left for this." She said, "Magpie, I believe you do." And then, as if she thought that this would please me, she added, "You clarify your skin and I guarantee you'll have Lazarus Goforth trailing you like a lovesick puppy."

Well, I can think of nothing worse. Lazarus is my cousin—one of Thelma's five brothers. Lazarus loves to fish. If he were to court me, he'd bring me fish to eat.

I hate fish.

I don't like fishing either.

I blow fish bubbles in my sticky bathwater. My hair fans out around me, getting caught up in the iron collar Big Mama's clamped around my slender neck. The collar's attached to a long iron chain. It starts at a ring in the floor of our Hidey-Hole. It snakes up the Hidey-Hole ramp, around the table in the front room, through the back room and into the kitchen where I float in Big Mama's large washing tub.

"I have to do this," Big Mama had said when she held me down and chained me up. This was after Wild Bill had thundered off, Randall had hobbled away to get his Horny Heads and Big Mama had hauled me to our cabin. "I have no choice. I'm the Keeper of Gabbard Mountain Law. You know that law—NO FEMALES NOR BOYS UNDER THE AGE OF EIGHTEEN IS ALLOWED OFF GABBARD MOUNTAIN AND THAT IS THAT."

"I didn't go off-mountain," I said.

"You was trying to," she said.

"I only wanted to see Milo." I said nothing about taking him his foot—still in my apron, hanging in this kitchen. While I managed to tear up the note I'd left—saying *I mean to visit my brother Milo and give him back his foot*—I've yet to get that foot back onto its Hallowed Spot.

"You'll see Milo when he comes home to his mama. Until then, you're chained to this cabin," she said.

"You can't do that!" I wailed.

"Oh yes I can," she said.

She's off now churning butter in the springhouse while I float chained in sticky water.

Coming up for air, I see, through our kitchen window, the waning moon. I often see her in the early morning sky, but never as late as it is now—close to midmorning. She should have set by now. Is she holding vigil with me? Well I'll be. She's worried about me. I wave to her through the window. Then I blow her a farewell kiss—to let her know that I'm all right. She can leave. I'll escape this chain. I'll return Milo's foot to him by the time he needs it.

Ain't I Margaret Magpie Gabbard?

Cussedness—that ability to find a way out of no way—comes with the name.

Chapter Nine

The Gabbard Chain of Sorrows

The moon's gone now. She's no doubt up in High Jerusalem—resting on her velvet throne. We won't see her for a night, maybe even two. They'll be dark nights, full of prowling Goblins. But I know the moon will return to once more bless us Gabbards with her loving light and keep us safe from them wicked creatures of the dark.

The moon always returns.

Unlike Milo.

I'm still floating in my honey bath. The bathwater's growing cold. I already hollered to Big Mama—back from churning and now getting ready for my party—"It's time for me to get out of this bathtub." She hollered back, "Have you clarified your skin?" I hollered, "No I haven't. But if you don't let

27

me out now, my skin will rot. All my black and white hair will fall out. I'll be even uglier than before. You want that for my thirteenth birthday?"

She didn't answer.

She cottons to her role of Mountain Jailer. Grandpa Gabbard knew she would. That's why he bequeathed the role to her instead of to his own son, my Sweet Daddy.

Sweet Daddy's too kind to lock up anyone.

The collar Big Mama clamped on me is the same one she used on Milo—to keep him from leaving us. The collar's attached to that iron chain I mentioned earlier—THE GABBARD CHAIN OF SORROWS. Grandpa forged all but one link in the chain. He'd be forging links still if he hadn't up and left. It was the strangest thing. One moment, my grandpa, who'd been ailing for some time, was lying in bed talking to me about the glories of High Jerusalem—the place he planned to be moving on to next. Grandpa said, "Magpie, there won't be no Sizemores in High Jerusalem. They ain't got a speck of good in them, so God won't let them in."

We both ruminated on that.

Then Grandpa said, "Magpie, come close. Look into my eyes and you'll see what I'm seeing—High Jerusalem's Pearly Gates."

As I was about to lean in and do just that, a look of horror crossed my grandpa's face and he shrieked, "Lord have mercy! What's Wiley Sizemore doing at them gates?"

Then came the greatest sorrow. Grandpa clutched his chest and died. Moments later, I saw his spirit, white as snow, leave his body, walk through our cabin window and then up the crystal staircase into the sky. It was then I truly understood what High Jerusalem was. It wasn't a place on earth. It was a place up there in heaven—a place that would make Grandpa and his aching bones happy while making me and my aching heart sad.

I cried and I cried.

Grandpa left us all his chain. Each link in it stands for a sorrow in the life of us Gabbards. We've got so many sorrows (and almost every one of them is the fault of them Sizemores) that if I was to sit knee to knee with my cousin Thelma, we could sing verses about them sorrows all the day and into the night.

The first sorrow came about because of lightning. Twenty-five years ago, lightning burned a hole in Wiley Sizemore's fence, which separated his corn crop from Grandpa's grazing field. This was when Grandpa had his farm alongside Wiley's—just outside Squabble Town.

The next five links are for Grandpa's dead cows. Them poor cows wandered through the new hole in Wiley's fence. They ate up Wiley's corn and that no-good Wiley shot them.

Well, Grandpa challenged Wiley to a duel. The up-shot being they each took a bullet in their shooting arms—after which neither was good for doing anything for sixty-seven days. Grandpa devoted sixty-seven sorrow links to that and rightly so.

Then you got the nineteen shoot-outs between our family and Wiley's, during which time us Gabbards could scarcely breathe for fear of getting fired upon. In them shoot-outs, no one got hit. No one died. Grandpa said, "What a waste of powder and shot!"

Grandpa forged nineteen sorrow links for that.

After this, Hopewell County was set up with Squabble Town as its seat and an election was held for a county sheriff. Wiley decided to run for the position. Grandpa did, too. He was certain he'd win because my grandpa had a plan—that being, he'd give a free gourd full of honey to anyone who'd vote for him.

Didn't he have a reputation for his honey?

YOU CAN'T HAVE A TASTE OF GABBY GABBARD'S HONEY WITHOUT WANTING MORE AND IT'S REAL GOOD FOR YOUR TEETH—that's what people said.

Thirty Sizemores promised to vote for my grandpa. Them sneaky Sizemores took his honey with a smile and then went on to vote for Wiley. Grandpa lost the election by thirty votes! On account of that, Grandpa added thirty more links to the Sorrow Chain. Grandpa told Wiley, "You and your kin will never taste my honey again."

Grandpa didn't want no Sheriff Wiley sniffing up his tail, so Grandpa upped his stakes. He moved his family five miles away from Squabble Town and up and onto Gabbard Mountain—the place where I was born and have lived my entire life and am floating in a tub of honey-water now.

But sorrows can come to you wherever you live.

Up here on our rolling plateau of a mountaintop, twenty-two links have been added to the Sorrow Chain. Twenty of them links concern the War between the States in which thieving Yankee soldiers (allied with Sizemores—dirty Yanks one and all) stole five of our hams, ten chickens, two cows, our entire corn crop and two mules. We nearly starved to death on top of which the South lost its Noble Cause for Independence.

The twenty-first sorrow is for Elmer Gabbard, Grandpa's brother, who, being chased out of Squabble

Town by Sizemores, hightailed it through Cob Hollow on a moonless night and Goblins got him.

And then you got the twenty-second sorrow—Milo. Grandpa being gone, Big Mama forged that link. It's the sorrow closest to my heart.

I'm tempted to escape this chain that holds me back from getting to my brother by doing what he finally had to—chopping off a limb.

Only Milo was chained up at the ankle.

I'm collared at the neck.

Chapter Ten

Them Goblins

ig Mama makes our clothes from wool off her sheep. Mostly she dyes them clothes dark purple. But she does have special dyes she uses for party colors. Them dyes come from dried snail spit, maple bark, leaf juices and Dorf Bug scales. I've always been partial to the orange color that comes from Dorf Bug scales. Big Mama knows this. So you'd think for my thirteenth birthday, with everyone coming here this afternoon to celebrate and me with my skin dried up from a honey bath that didn't do no good, Big Mama would at least have made me a dress in my favorite color. But she hasn't. The dress Big Mama's now buttoning onto me is white. I don't know how she got the cloth to be so white, but she did and it's dull-ugly.

She calls the color, "wedding-white."

I call it, "maggot-white."

"It accentuates my pimple-spots. I still got all seven of them. I counted," I tell Big Mama, now fastening the final dress button at the back of my slender neck—still collared and with that Sorrow Chain, like a heavy iron tail, hanging down my back.

"The dress accentuates your hair," Big Mama says. "You have your Great-Grandmother Margaret's beautiful black and white hair."

"Yes I do." I also got something else my great-grandmother had—something tailing me—this Chain of Sorrows. It goes *clankety-clank* across the floor as I proceed to get out dishes for my birthday celebration and Big Mama goes into the kitchen to make up apple fizz to serve with my cake.

Great-Grandmother had a different kind of tail—hers was a long chain of Goblins. That's how the stories go. They say Goblins followed her here all the way from England. They slunk into Cob Hollow—that dark narrow valley between Squabble Town and Gabbard Mountain—and made its marl pits and bog holes their home.

Why did they follow Great-Grandmother here?

No one knows.

But we all know this. Goblins love the dark—the kind you find on moonless nights when you can't see where you're going. On these nights, Goblins swarm out of Cob Hollow. They prowl the slopes of Gabbard Mountain and all through the streets of Squabble Town, too. If you dare go outside on these nights, you'll be in mortal danger. Goblins, hunched over as they creep along, will tail you. They'll whisper to you one of their terrifying rhymes, hoping to scare you into doing something foolish, like stumbling into a marl pit, and then, they'll grab you up.

On moonless nights, I've heard their whisperings seeping through chinks in our cabin wall:

> *And we'll beat you, beat you, beat you,*
> *And we'll beat you all to pap,*
> *And we'll eat you, eat you, eat you,*
> *Every morsel, snap, snap, snap.*

Them fool Goblins. They recite that rhyme about eating folks when we all know they do something far worse. They suck folks dry and then fill them up with Goblin rotgut, thereby turning them into one of their own.

We got thousands upon thousands of Goblins lurking near the foot of Gabbard Mountain—just waiting for moonless nights to come along so that they can leave their hollow and terrorize us all.

Chapter Eleven

Milo's Foot

I trudge into the kitchen—dragging my chain tail across the wood plank floor—*clankety-clank-clank.* "Just getting my apron," I tell Big Mama, who's at the sink, peeling apples. I put the apron on. Back in the front room, I slip Milo's foot out of the pocket. I place the foot back onto its Hallowed Spot on the mantle so Big Mama won't know I tried to steal it. If she were to find that out, I'd be in more trouble than I already am.

Even though this foot can't talk, I know it's dying to be reunited with my brother. Look at this foot. It stubbornly holds on to life even though it's been apart from Milo for over six weeks now. I tell you, the foot's got grit. There ain't nothing like grit. Grit gives you the wherewithall to keep on with what you're doing, even though it's hard, and it seems impossible and you feel like giving up.

Tears flood my eyes as I brush past the chair where Milo used to sit—his dog Talker at his feet. Milo named him Talker because that dog talked to my brother. When Milo was too sick to get up from bed, he'd ask Talker, "What's the weather like?" Talker would trot out the door. Moments later, he'd be back. Talker would tell Milo one of two things—either, "Too hot to chase rabbits," or, "Too cold." Then he'd curl up in the place he loved the best—a nest he'd made in the blankets at my brother's side.

Talker loved it when Milo played his musical hands. A day never went by without Milo making trumpet music by squeezing air between them hands. For me Milo's music always eased an aching heart. If I could hear it now, it would make me forget this Chain of Sorrows I have to drag along with me. Milo's music was like birdsong in winter—making you smile with the hope of spring.

Why, Milo had grown so good at this kind of music making that this past August God Himself came to my brother. To my dying day, I'll remember Milo telling me about it. He'd come to me, all excited. He said, "Magpie, you might not believe me if I tell you this, but I got to tell someone. I was visited by God last night."

"What? By God Himself?" I said.

"Yes," Milo said. "God Himself. He invited me to play my hands at High Jerusalem's Fall Jubilee on October sixteenth. He said all His saints and repentant sinners will be there, including our grandpa. God said I'll have a fine time. Afterward, I can go on to play my hands at High Jerusalem's Pearly Gates. God said my music will welcome in the weary travelers.

"I told God, 'I'd like that. I'd like it all. I'll pack my bags directly.' "

Having understood by now that going off to High Jerusalem meant Milo would climb the crystal staircase to the sky, leaving me with so much sorrow I couldn't bear it, I told him, "I don't care what God told you. I'm telling you this—you ain't going."

Milo said, "When God calls, it changes you. You can't stay where you are. You have to move on, but just think, Magpie. I'll get to play in his celestial band."

I said, "Don't go."

Milo said, "I have to."

I said, "No you don't."

We carried on like this for quite some time. I kept

Milo from leaving us for upward to a week. And then, late one hot afternoon, when Milo was feeling well enough to walk outside, he came to me—in secret. He hugged me. He said, "I'm leaving tomorrow at day-break. I couldn't go without telling you good-bye."

Well, I told Big Mama on him. She didn't want Milo leaving us neither. She loved him too much. And so, with Randall's help, she locked Milo up to the Chain of Sorrows while I looked on. I'll never forget the look I saw on Milo's face—*Magpie, how could you betray me?* Nor the sight of his foot the following morning—lying discarded alongside the chain.

Oh, that haunts me.

Milo's foot stayed here, while he, with the faithful Talker at his side, left Gabbard Mountain. But Milo didn't make it to High Jerusalem the way he'd planned. Instead, he and Talker ended up in faraway Purgatory, Kentucky—known for its high mountains, deep forests and giant hollowed-out sycamore trees.

Chapter Twelve

Purgatory

Now, I've never been to Purgatory although I did see it once—in Granny Goforth's prophesying kettle. It was a week after Milo had left us—a long, hot and miserable week. Our entire family—Gabbards and Goforths—had gathered around Granny's steaming kettle. When Granny shouted, "Kettle, show us Milo, where is he?" we saw a giant hollowed-out sycamore tree—the kind that's only found in Purgatory—a tree so big inside you could make a home out of it. A stream cut through the stony ground in front of this tree. A high mountain ridge rose behind. And there was Milo, leaning against the sycamore because, by then, he only had one foot to stand on.

My heart leaped when I saw him.

I leaned into the kettle. I wanted to touch my brother. Granny said, "No, Magpie. The kettle water's steaming hot. You'll get burnt. Besides, what you see in the water ain't Milo in the flesh. It's just a picture of him."

In that picture, Milo was playing his musical hands. His dog Talker lay nearby—his chin pressed to the ground. Talker, who always liked to sing with Milo's music, wasn't singing now. His paws covered his ears. This and the pained expression on Milo's face told me—told us all—*something here's not right.* Probably that something's what landed him in Purgatory.

Sweet Daddy headed off to find out what was going on with Milo and bring him home. After a considerable journey, Sweet Daddy found my brother. By this time, Milo was living inside that hollowed-out sycamore we'd seen in Granny's kettle. He had a bed of leaves in there, along with a wood chair, a stone fireplace he'd built and Talker for company.

Milo played "Down by the Riverside" for Sweet Daddy while Talker cringed. Later, Sweet Daddy told me that Milo's music was the awfullest thing he'd ever heard. He said, "It was the first time in my life I'd ever heard your brother play off-key."

Milo knew he sounded awful.

He told Sweet Daddy, "I can't be playing at God's Jubilee with notes gone sour. I've got to get them right."

"You should come on home with me," Sweet Daddy said.

Milo said, "You know I can't go back. God's called me. I'll stay here and practice 'til I get it right."

"What if you don't get it right in time for His Fall Jubilee?" Sweet Daddy said.

"Then I reckon I'll be stuck in Purgatory forever," Milo said. "I'll dry up here. There won't be nothing left of me but a shell."

When Sweet Daddy told me this, it broke my heart.

I asked Sweet Daddy, "Do you reckon if Milo had two feet to stand on instead of one, it would even him out so that he could play in tune?" I said it softly because I didn't want Big Mama to hear. She'd never allow Milo to have his foot. By holding on to it, she thinks she's holding on to him.

Sweet Daddy whispered back, "Why, Magpie, I reckon it would."

Chapter Thirteen

Sweet Daddy

What's that I hear now? Why, it's my own Sweet Daddy—outside this cabin and calling to his hogs—"Come on, my pretty ones. It's Magpie's birthday. We're having a party. Trot along, Sadie. Sissy, look smart." I swear there ain't a kinder man on earth than my Sweet Daddy. He names all his hogs. He treats them like family.

I prop open the door to the Hidey-Hole. Then I fling wide the cabin door so Sweet Daddy's hogs can trot right in. And what am I greeted by? Fog! When did that thick fog settle in? Fog's so sudden. One moment it ain't here. The next it is.

Seven black and white hogs trot out of that fog. In single file, they trot up the cabin steps, across the front porch, through the open door and down the ramp into the Hidey-Hole where they know we'll keep them safe from Goblins for the entire night. Goblins don't suck out a hog's blood and replace it with their own—the way they will a human. But they will eat hogs. Goblins will eat anything alive.

And here's Sweet Daddy, stepping in behind the last of his hogs, a panting dog on either side of him. A sad look comes over Sweet Daddy at seeing me collared and chained. He hates the Chain of Sorrows. If he'd been home that time I'd told on Milo, Sweet Daddy never would have locked my brother up. But Sweet Daddy had been off-mountain buying salt and coffee beans.

"Look what Big Mama's done to me and on my thirteenth birthday!" I wail.

Sweet Daddy opens his arms and I throw myself into them. He staggers to gain his balance, but that don't stop him from holding on and hugging me. His orange coat smells of hog and tobacco smoke. I love him to pieces.

"Why'd Big Mama chain you?" Sweet Daddy says.

"I tried to leave our mountain. I only wanted to

see Milo. Just for the day." I don't say nothing about the foot.

"I rode Wild Bill," I tell Sweet Daddy.

"You did?" Sweet Daddy rears back in my arms so's he can look me in the eye. I look him direct right back. He says, "How long did you sit the boar?"

"I'd say a good five minutes."

"Well, I'll be." Sweet Daddy runs his hand through the white streak in my hair. He loves my white streak. He says the color reminds him of his special friend—the moon.

"If Randall hadn't fired his shotgun—making Wild Bill turn so hard I flew over his head—that boar would have carried me to Milo. I'd have shared my thirteenth birthday with my favorite brother. After which, I'd have come back home to you—all on this single, special day." This is almost the entire truth.

"You miss Milo." Sweet Daddy draws me, collar, chain and all, back into his arms. I rest my cheek against his rough wool coat.

I say, "I miss him so much my heart aches."

Sweet Daddy rests his chin on top of my head. He says, "I've been thinking about what I should give you for your thirteenth birthday. As I was searching out my hogs, I asked myself, 'What would Magpie want?' I looked up at the early morning sky. I saw the moon—up there so high above us all. And I heard her lovely voice inside my heart. The moon said, 'Sweets, what Magpie wants most is to see her brother. Once I'm back from my rest and it's safe for you to travel, take her to him.' "

"The moon said that? What about THE LAW—NO FEMALES NOR BOYS UNDER THE AGE OF EIGHTEEN IS ALLOWED OFF GABBARD MOUNTAIN AND THAT IS THAT?"

"I talked to the moon about that, too," Sweet Daddy says. He's always one for talking to the moon. "We both agree—that law has caused us Gabbards more harm than good."

"So you'll take me to see Milo?" Now it's me rearing back in Sweet Daddy's arms.

He says, "I will and that's a promise. We'll leave tomorrow."

"Sweet Daddy, that's the best birthday present a girl could ask for." I hug him so hard, I'm like to bust.

"You're taking Magpie off-mountain to see Milo?" Big Mama roars into our faces. When did she come into the room? For a large woman, Big Mama sure moves quiet—too quiet.

"I'll take you both," Sweet Daddy tells her.

"You'll do this in spite of THE LAW—made to keep

us on Gabbard Mountain where we'll be safe from the OUTSIDE WORLD WITH ITS PERNICIOUS SIZEMORES?" she says.

"I will," Sweet Daddy says.

"Then what's the use of THAT LAW?" she says.

"There ain't none. I never thought there was although my daddy did." By "daddy" he means my Grandpa Gabbard.

"Well, I'll be." Big Mama bites her knuckles the way she will when pondering. "If there's no use for that law, then why should it exist?"

"It shouldn't," Sweet Daddy says.

"I've been enforcing that law for months." She stares at him. He stares right back.

I reckon now she's gonna storm out of here and have herself a sulk because how can she leave this mountain when she's just locked me up for trying? Instead, she sighs. And then, she smiles. And then, she hauls Sweet Daddy out of my loving arms and into hers! "Sweets, you've made me the happiest woman alive." She hugs him hard. "I can see Milo. Magpie can see Milo. Randall can see Milo. Randall misses his brother.

"Randall ain't been the same since Milo fled. None of us has. We'll bring Milo home! We'll be a big family once again. Come here, Magpie." Big Mama draws me, chain and all, into her and Sweet Daddy's hug. We have us a BIG WARM BEAR HUG. I have an urge to say, "You know Milo can't come home." But I realize this might cause an argument. We don't need an argument at this time.

Chapter Fourteen

A Reversal
in Fortune

Sweet Daddy, Big Mama and I have us the longest BEAR HUG in what I believe must be Gabbard Mountain history. I grow hot from all the body heat. I finally tear myself away in order to cool off and that's when I hear singing coming from outside our cabin. It's them Goforths—coming to celebrate my birthday. Them Goforths love to sing. They can carry on for hours. Only today, as they draw ever nearer, I can tell they're not singing the particular song meant for a gal's thirteenth birthday—that being:

Birthday gal, won't you come out tonight?
Come out tonight? Come out tonight?

Birthday gal, won't you come out tonight?
And dance by the light of the moon.

Nope. They're singing a fare-thee-well song—
meant for someone dead or dying. These are the sorry
words that now assail our ears and set Big Mama to
shrieking, "Lord have mercy—something's happened
to my other son":

Farewell, dear Randall, you're bound
  for glory,
Soon you'll reach the Promised Land.
We'll sorely miss your jokes and laughter,
We're sad your eating got out of hand.

Did Randall's out-of-hand eating have anything to
do with his eating Horny Heads? I told Thelma to
only use a pinch of Bug Dirt for the seasoning! Did
she use more? Am I about to suffer from what
Grandpa Gabbard has called our family curse—"The
Reversal in Fortune"?

And here everything had started to turn in
my favor.

We make a stampede for the cabin door, Big Mama
in the lead. I drag the Gabbard Chain of Sorrows. It

clangs along behind me, playing a mournful song. Big Mama flings wide the door and what are we greeted by? A fog grown so thick, you can't see through it!

"Where's my boy?" Big Mama waves her hand—trying to clear away the fog.

"Come on, Rosie. We'll find him." Sweet Daddy grabs hold of Big Mama's waving hand. Hand in hand, they head down the front steps, leaving me alone—forgetting I'm confined to the porch by the Sorrow Chain. From somewhere in the thick fog ahead, them Goforths sing the same sorry song over and over as they draw ever nearer to the cabin.

I squint my eyes, trying to sharpen my vision so that I can see what's going on. Through the fog, I can just make out the dark branches of our oak tree, looming forth above the spot where Big Mama and Sweet Daddy have just disappeared into fog. And then, all of a sudden, I see something so peculiar it almost takes my breath away.

I see Randall's head. I can't see the rest of him on account of the fog. But I do see his head. I hope it's still attached to something. It bobs through the fog toward me in time to the Goforths' singing and the solemn creak of wagon wheels.

"This ain't Thelma's fault!" Aunt Louisa—that's

Thelma's mama—screeches from somewhere in the thick fog near Randall's head. She must be walking somewhere near that head. She screeches, "Thelma cooked up them Horny Heads real nice!"

I just bet she did.

As Randall draws ever nearer, I see his head's still attached to his neck and his neck to his body—a relief. His black hair sticks straight out the same way the fur on Sweet Daddy's hound dogs did that day they ate Bug Dirt. Randall sits bolt upright in Uncle Henry's ladder-back chair that's being hauled along inside Uncle Henry's wagon—pulled by his mule that's being driven by Aunt Louisa. Randall clutches a large fried Horny Head in his right hand—that hand about to put the fish's head into his mouth.

It looks like Randall froze up solid in midbite.

Do I know who caused this? I believe I do. Here she comes now—leaping out of the fog and up onto the porch—Thelma. Her brown hair's frizzed up and her wide blue eyes filled with terror.

"Magpie! You didn't tell me Bug Dirt would freeze up Randall!" Thelma hisses at me.

"I didn't know it would." I watch them five Goforth brothers now lift a clearly paralyzed Randall from the wagon. Big Mama bustles around him shrieking, "Randall's breathing! Randall's alive! At least he's alive!" Them Goforths carry Randall—fish, chair and all—past Thelma and me and into the cabin.

I don't believe this. All I wanted for my birthday was to take Milo his foot and now I'm chained up and with a frozen Randall, too. I pull Thelma aside. "How much Bug Dirt did you use on them Horny Heads?"

"The entire handful. You told me it would sweeten him up and it did—until he froze in midbite," she whimpers.

"I told you to use a pinch!" I hiss.

"I know. But he kept telling me to pour on the seasoning, so I did—along with a handful of salt. Randall does love salt.

"I didn't know it would make him sick." Tears well in Thelma's eyes.

"Oh, stop your sniffling. Eating Bug Dirt never killed anyone." I remind myself that we have a cure for its ill-effects as well—Green Water. Sweet Daddy used that on his dogs. "What we need to worry about is Sweet Daddy. Soon enough, he'll figure out what's behind Randall's frozen state. Fingers will be pointed at you."

"You gave the Bug Dirt to me." Thelma punches my arm.

"You poured it on." I punch her back. "You couldn't be satisfied with a pinch. You had to use the entire handful. To top it off, you poured on salt. Too much salt's bad for anyone. You know that.

"Thelma!" I find myself shrieking her name. "Do you know what? You poured Sizemore salt on them Horny Heads you served Randall." Everyone knows the Sizemores own the only salt well in the county.

"Yes I did. My daddy bought that Sizemore salt just yesterday at the Squabble Town Store." Thelma wipes her nose.

"Thelma, them Sizemores poisoned that salt with Bug Dirt," I say.

"No they didn't, Magpie—we did!" she says.

"Now you listen to me." I pinch Thelma's right ear so's she will. *They poisoned the salt with Bug Dirt.*"

"Why'd they do that?" she says.

"Didn't they kill Grandpa's cows? Didn't they ruin his shooting arm? Didn't they cause him to lose the election for sheriff? He could have been county sheriff!" I list these twenty-five-year-old wounds that, in our hearts, are still fresh and festering.

"Thelma." I pinch her ear a little harder. "Them Sizemores have caused us trouble from the get-go.

We may as well blame this latest trouble on them. Because if Big Mama were to find out the truth—that you and I poisoned Randall—she'd skin us and nail our hides up on the outside of the barn to dry."

And I'd never see Milo again.

"You want that, Thelma?" I say.

Chapter Fifteen

Green Water

Randall sits frozen-like in Uncle Henry's chair, which them Goforth brothers have placed in front of our fire in hopes the heat might loosen Randall up. Everyone on Gabbard Mountain has gathered around my brother except for Granny Goforth. She's out in her shed, consulting with her prophesying kettle. Granny wants to find out who or what's behind my brother's sudden froze-up state.

I hope she don't find out it's Thelma and me.

Thelma's arm butts up against mine—two cousins against the world. "Randall ate five of my Horny Heads," Thelma is saying. "He was about to eat that sixth when he froze up." Sweet Daddy, on his knees, is trying to pry the sixth fish out of Randall's hand.

Randall can't seem to let it go.

"I caught them Horny Heads myself," Lazarus says. He's the Goforth that Big Mama's fixing to court me. Lazarus purses his thick lips and shakes his head at Randall's sorrowful state. "Them fish was fresh," he says. "I didn't let them hang too long in the sun. Nor did I let them flop in the dirt. I swear."

"I believe you, Lazarus," I say.

"You do?" he says.

As much as it pains me, for I don't want to encourage his advances, I nod my head. "What's behind Randall's sorrowful state ain't the fish themselves. It's the poisoned salt that Thelma put on them."

"I didn't poison that salt!" Thelma screams at me.

"I know you didn't," I say. "Them Sizemores did. Everyone knows—you buy salt at the Squabble Town Store, it's Sizemore salt—straight from Duck Sizemore's salt well."

"You're saying Duck Sizemore poisoned that salt I bought?" Uncle Henry—he's Thelma's daddy—says.

"Yes I am," I say.

"A passel of folks bought salt that day. I can't imagine Duck wanting to poison any of them—in particular his Sizemore kin," Uncle Henry says.

"Duck didn't poison their salt—just yours," I say.

"How did he manage to do that?" Uncle Henry says.

"Them Sizemores have their ways," I say.

"Indeed they do," Big Mama chimes in. "Them Sizemore ways have brought us more sorrows than links on Grandpa Gabbard's Chain."

I rattle the chain that I'm still wearing.

"That chain looks heavy." Buck, the oldest of the five Goforth brothers, tugs on it. I swipe at him and Randall belches. A sickening smell—like a dozen rotted eggs broke open—fills the air.

"I'd know that smell anywhere! My son's eaten Bug Dirt!" Sweet Daddy rises to his feet.

"Duck Sizemore poisoned the salt with Bug Dirt!" I state this like a pronouncement from ON HIGH.

"I don't know if Duck's behind this or not." Sweet Daddy looks straight on at me. Does he recall the time he showed me the pile of Bug Dirt his dogs had got into so's I wouldn't try eating the same dirt myself?

How could he not?

His gaze travels from my reddening face, to my collared neck, to the Chain of Sorrows hanging down my back.

I never should have fooled with Bug Dirt.

He says, "What's important right now is that I know a cure." He wipes his hands on his overalls and then he reaches into Big Mama's apron pocket. He brings out the iron key to the Gabbard Chain.

"What do you want with my key?" Big Mama says.

"I mean to free our Magpie." He unlocks the collar from around my neck. The Chain of Sorrows clatters to the floor.

He says, "Magpie, I want you to crawl your way through those piles of books beneath your grandpa's bed and find his flask of Green Water. It cured my dogs of Bug Dirt poisoning. It should cure Randall, too.

"Magpie, can you fetch that Green Water for me?"

"Yes sir, I can." *Sweet Daddy's set me free.* I make a beeline for my grandpa's room off our back porch. I've heard that Green Water, which comes from a pond in Eastern Tennessee, got its healing power from the love in a young girl's heart for a boy she could never have. In order to save the boy's life, she had to love him hard enough to let him go.

I don't know all the story of that love and the letting go and how it came to make a cure-all, but I can tell you this. My Sweet Daddy loves me; I love him back so much, my heart's about to bust.

Chapter Sixteen

A Reversal in Fortune Part Two

reen Water, which my grandpa would buy from Doc Buckle who lives in Squabble Town, is a powerful cure-all. It restores sight to the blind, relieves itchy scalps and is, of course, the antidote to Bug Dirt poisoning. On top of all this, it eased my grandpa's bouts of angry indigestion, brought on each time he saw the Sorrow Chain and recollected all the wrongs them Sizemores done him.

Grandpa must have been real angry before he left us this past July for High Jerusalem. He must have had himself several indigestion fits. Because the flask of Green Water I now find tucked among his multi-volume set of *The History of the Decline and Fall of the Roman Empire* is empty.

"Grandpa drained the flask dry. There's no Green

Water left. Not even a drop," I tell everyone in the front room. I tip the flask upside down so they can see the terrible truth for themselves. The Reversal in Fortune that I noted earlier seems to be continuing on a downward spiral.

"What do we do now?" Big Mama wails.

"I'll fetch more Green Water!" Sweet Daddy grabs his hog rifle—setting by the door. "I'll be back with it before you know I'm gone."

"You can't make it down the mountain, through Cob Hollow, into Squabble Town, over to Doc's and then be back again before nightfall," Aunt Louisa tells him. She's his sister—known for saying things as they are and not as we'd like them to be. I never did cotton much to Aunt Louisa because of this, but I do now. *I don't want Sweet Daddy to go.*

"You can't be traveling after nightfall," Big Mama tells Sweet Daddy.

"There's no moon," Aunt Louisa says.

"The Goblins will get you," Buck says.

"Wait until tomorrow," I say.

"I can't wait. Look at Randall," Sweet Daddy says.

We all turn to my brother. His entire face has now gone buttercup yellow. I can't help but gasp. This is far worse than anything I could imagine.

"If I leave now, I'll be back before dark." Whistling

for his dogs, Sweet Daddy heads out the door. His black hair curls where it hits the shoulders of his orange coat. He's got a lift to his step in spite of being out all day with the hogs. I run after him. I stop him on the porch. I say, "Sweet Daddy, I should go with you. It's the least I can do. Randall's being poisoned is at least partly my fault. I know you know that."

"What I expect you did was dead wrong, but it ain't all your fault. Something larger and more troublesome than you fighting with your brother has us Gabbards in its grip.

"Stay here. Help Big Mama with Randall. We'll talk when I get back." Sweet Daddy runs his hand along the moon white streak in my hair—the way he will for luck. I take his hand and fold his fingers over—locking that luck inside. Not Sweet Daddy nor I say anything about Milo. I hope he's biding his time and practicing his music in that sycamore tree. I reckon Sweet Daddy does, too.

Chapter Seventeen

That Infernal Fog

This cabin feels dark and gloomy without Sweet Daddy here. He's been gone for almost two hours—it seems like years. Them five Goforth brothers now sit with Uncle Henry at my birthday table. They sing a mournful ballad in harmony—"Jimmy Randal." It's an unfortunate choice of song to Thelma's and my way of thinking. It concerns a man poisoned by his sweetheart and he died.

Nearby, Big Mama and Aunt Louisa pore over a book Aunt Louisa thought to bring along with her—THE FAMILY NURSE. They're trying to come up with something to tide Randall over until Sweet Daddy returns with the Green Water.

Randall's entire body's now turned yellow.

A somber-faced Thelma and I serve the singing

men and consulting mamas their honey cake and apple fizz. Back in the kitchen, I cut Thelma and me some cake. I pour our drinks. We sit at the sawbuck table. I tell Thelma, "My thirteenth birthday ain't turning out the way I'd planned."

She says, "They never do. Remember mine? All I wanted was for Randall to give me a diamond sparkle for the fourth finger of my left hand." Thelma waves that finger in front of my face. "Instead, he gave me nothing. I ain't fond of nothing.

"You know what, Magpie?" she says.

"What's that, Thelma?" I hope she don't still want that sparkle.

"Smelling Randall's belch brought to mind that time he put stinky beetles down my back when I was ten years old. I don't want to marry him now."

"He wasn't right for you anyway." And that's the truth. Randall was always playing tricks on Thelma. To him, she was more of a pesky sister than a sweetheart.

"Who's left on this mountain to court me?" she says.

"No one," I say.

We ponder that.

Thelma asks for a second piece of cake. I give it to

her, saying, "This is your final piece, Thelma. I'm saving the rest for Sweet Daddy."

"Think he's made it through Cob Hollow by now?" The quickest way to Doc's is through that hollow.

"He's through it, been to Doc's, and by now, he's hoofing it back up our mountain." Doc's is only five miles away and Sweet Daddy can run real fast.

"I wish that fog would clear off." Thelma stares out the window. "It looks like dusk out there. If your Sweet Daddy gets caught in Cob Hollow at dusk, he'll never come back."

"We got time before dusk, Thelma."

"Might as well be nighttime." She keeps looking out that window.

"But it ain't. Now hush up. You're irritating me." We sit in silence. Thelma finishes her cake. She licks cake crumbs off her fingertips one by one. She's down to her final pinky finger when a faraway sound assails our senses—

THWOCK! THWOCK! THWOCK!

Goblins. We can hear them from clear up here on our mountaintop. A Goblin lifts its ugly head from the Cob Hollow muck—THWOCK! It lifts an arm—THWOCK! It lifts another arm—THWOCK! It pulls out its entire body—THWOCK! THWOCK! THWOCK! Multiply them THWOCKS by the hundreds of thousands of Goblins we got lurking in Cob Hollow and you'll get an idea of the racket that now assaults our ears and strikes terror in our hearts.

Thelma stares at me. She don't say, "I told you it felt like dusk." She grabs my hand and squeezes it. I squeeze hers back. Sweet Daddy had better be through Cob Hollow! He'd better be hightailing it back up our mountain—NOW!

Chapter Eighteen

Cob Hollow

In sunny daylight, on a happy day say in June, when spring's still got a green hold on our mountain, you might forget—at least for a moment—that them Goblins exist. They hide out so quiet-like in Cob Hollow, with its deep marl pits, giant boulders, swampy undergrowth, dark pools and fir trees that keep the place in constant shadow.

But them Goblins are there.

If you travel through Cob Hollow on that sunny day—on your way from Gabbard Mountain to Squabble Town to do some trading—you just might spy two red eyes glaring at you from a deep pool of muddy water in which a Goblin's hiding from the light. And even though you know that Goblin won't come out after you—not with all the sunlight—still, you'll hug yourself and hurry onward . . . down, down, down the narrow twisting path that winds all through the hollow.

You'll skirt the marl pits. You'll hurry around giant boulders. You'll wade through the low swampy areas further on. And then, just before you hit the swinging bridge that will take you into Squabble Town, you'll find yourself up against a dense clutch of fir trees—the Hall of the Goblin King. You'd better run through that for all you're worth. For the shadows here are darker than pitch. The Goblin King, wearing his crown of human finger bones, holds court in them shadows.

Once, Grandpa Gabbard didn't run through that Hall. He walked as brazen as you please—until he felt sharp fingernails on the back of his neck.

Goblins are a fearful thing! The sound they make as they now rise from their murky lairs sends us Gabbard Mountain folk into a tizzy. Big Mama and I have to prepare our cabin for the night. As for them Goforths, they need to head out for their farm.

They have to:

1. Get home—it's a twenty-minute wagon ride across our flat-topped mountain to their farm on the other side.

2. Bring in Granny from her consultation shed, which is out behind the Goforths' barn.
3. Bring in the Horny Heads that Lazarus hung out on the line to dry.
4. Call the animals into the cabin for safe-keeping.
5. Build up the night fires.
6. Lock the doors and windows tight.

And all within the hour.

By then, the Goblins will be here.

In the front room, folks grab up their coats and hats while Aunt Louisa gives Big Mama last-minute instructions concerning Randall—still frozen, still yellow. While Thelma and I were eating cake in the kitchen, Aunt Louisa and Big Mama found a treatment for Randall in *The Family Nurse*.

This is that treatment:

Randall must drink, without fail, a full cup of brown lye soap dissolved in warm water every four minutes until the scouring soap has its effect and he erupts, whereby he'll throw up any remaining Bug Dirt in his system. This won't cure Randall. But it should keep his condition from growing worse.

There ain't nothing worse than the taste of lye

soap. I should know. I've had my mouth scrubbed out with it more times than I care to count—for bad-mouthing one thing or another.

"What about the Green Water Sweet Daddy's bringing home? It'll cure Randall on the spot," I tell Aunt Louisa, now throwing on her shawl.

"That Green Water ain't here," she says in that no-nonsense way she has. "The lye soap is."

Chapter Nineteen

Making Our Own Light

I don't hear them THWOCKS no more. This means the Goblins have left their lairs. They're swarming across the countryside—up mountain and down. Soon a passel of them will show up here. They always do. I have to get the cabin lit and ready to face them.

In my room, I change out of my thirteenth birthday dress and into my old purple one. I slip on my apron. It feels sadly empty without Milo's foot weighing it down. His foot hasn't given up on life. I mustn't either.

In the front room, Big Mama tends to Randall—feeding him soapy water. I throw pine knots on the hearth fire. I get it blazing hot and bright enough to light the entire room. If a Goblin peers into our front window, it'll see we got enough light in here to burn it blind.

I head into the back room. Here, next to the window, the afternoon sun, day after day, has baked the chinking in the log wall as brittle as a dead man's fingernails. Them Goblins like to pick at that chinking—*pickety pick.* Trying to pick a hole big enough so's they can scuttle their long bony hands through and up the inside of the window to the latch. Then they'll open it, climb in and SUCK US DRY.

To stop them from even trying, I bring out the cow's skull that Milo and I found last spring. Milo, always one for bright ideas, had said, "What if we take this skull and put lit candles in its eye sockets? What if we place that in the back room window to stare out at them Goblins when they come a-picking?

"What do you think, Magpie?" Milo said.

I said, "I think it'll scare them silly."

And it did.

Because of that candle-lit cow skull, we didn't have to spend the night the way we used to—smashing off Goblin fingers with frying pans and throwing the finger bits onto the fire, where they burned, stinking up the cabin good and setting those Goblins into howling fit to die. Inside the cabin, we had the freedom to do as we pleased while Goblins hungrily prowled around outside until dawn. Big Mama could knit. Milo could make trumpet music, which, in spite of all the horror going on outside, always made us smile. Grandpa could read. Randall would feed the fire— Randall's always been right fond of fire. I'd rub Sweet Daddy's head. We'd sing ballads.

If only Sweet Daddy could be with us now. Where is he!

Chapter Twenty

Happier Times

It's getting on to midnight. My thirteenth birthday has almost ended. Sweet Daddy still ain't back. Big Mama and I now both agree—Sweet Daddy got waylaid by Doc. Doc loves to talk about the War between the States that left us starved and without a penny to our name. Doc no doubt talked Sweet Daddy to death, then, seeing how dark it had grown, Doc made Sweet Daddy stay over for the night.

That's where he was—at Doc's. Sweet Daddy would be home shortly after daylight.

I sit in Sweet Daddy's chair, placed firmly on the door to the Hidey-Hole, in which all our livestock now sleep except for the chickens—roosting in the loft. Goblins have settled on the rooftop. Our chickens are clucking up a fuss. Other Goblins pace back and forth across the front porch. I hear the floorboards squeak. I've got Big Mama's hog rifle stretched across my lap. If Goblins should try to rattle our door loose from its hinges and then hurl themselves into our cabin, I'll blow them to bits.

Big Mama has had her hands full with Randall. She's been feeding him soapy water for several hours now. Each time she gives him a cupful, she has to carefully work her hand around that Horny Head my brother won't let go of no matter what.

Randall's got so much soapy water inside him now, he can't hold it all. It overflows onto his chin. When Big Mama mops it up, she breaks the soap bubbles, releasing a stench strong enough to make me gag. Big Mama says this stench means the soap is having its desired effect—scouring out the Bug Dirt inside Randall—bubble by bubble.

I wish Randall would just erupt, spill out all that Bug Dirt and get it over with. I throw another pine knot on the fire. It spits—sending bright sparks up the chimney and into the night.

A Goblin peeks in our front window. I see its blood red eyes. It hisses:

Blow the fire and make the toast,
Put the babies on to roast,
Blow the fire and make the toast,
We'll all have tea.

"I can't take this no more!" Big Mama turns a tear-streaked face on me. When did she start crying? I hate it when she cries!

"Don't cry, Big Mama!" I rush over and I pat her back. She sets into sobbing.

Between sobs, she says, "My Sweets ain't back."

"Course he ain't back. He's at Doc's." *He has to be at Doc's.*

"I need him here. Randall's bubbling. We've got Goblins on the roof, at the window and on the porch. I want my Sweets!" Tears stream down Big Mama's cheeks. The last time she let loose like this was the morning we found Milo's foot on the front room floor and Milo gone. That was a terrible time. Which takes me to thinking about that precious brother in his sycamore tree.

Drawing in a deep breath, I take the wet cloth that Big Mama's been using to mop up Randall and I say, "Go on over by the fire and have yourself a smoke. I'll take care of Randall myself."

"You will?" Big Mama's surprise stops up her tears.

"Yes I will." I help Big Mama to a stand. Handing her the hog rifle, I settle down in the chair alongside my brother. Big Mama goes on over to her rocking chair. She sets down and lays the rifle across her lap. She reaches for her pipe. She tamps dried corn silk into the pipe bowl as I angle my hand around the fried Horny Head Randall's still got in a death grip. I haven't been this close to Randall in some time, unless you count them times he's grabbed hold of me in anger—them times that came after Milo left.

I don't see no anger in Randall tonight. I see gratefulness. As if Randall's grateful to me for cleaning him up. Well, I don't believe it. *Randall's grateful.* I find myself smiling at my brother. That smile causes me to recall out loud a happier time when I was little and he lifted me up onto his broad shoulders so's I could reach a dead ripe apple I was hungering to eat.

"You remember that, Randall?" I ask.

Randall blinks his eyes—he remembers.

Randall blinked his eyes.

"And then there was that time Milo thought up the wooden pipe system that brings water downhill from our well." If I keep talking about happier times, maybe I'll unfreeze more of Randall than his eyelids. "You remember that, Randall? You and I built that water system. Milo wasn't feeling too good, but still, he cheered us on. We got so excited when that water system worked. You, me, Milo—we whooped and hollered. No more hauling water into the kitchen day after tiresome day.

"Those were happy times, weren't they, Randall?" I say.

Randall agrees with me. His mouth, which had been open all this time in order to bite into that Horny Head, opens even wider.

To my surprise, a giant yellow-colored soap bubble now slowly issues forth from Randall's open mouth. It looks as if all the Bug Dirt in the world's inside that bubble.

I yell to Big Mama, "Something's coming out of Randall's mouth!" The bubble grows bigger and bigger until it's pumpkin-sized—at which point, it breaks off.

The giant bubble hovers over Randall's head.

"Don't let that bubble pop! It'll stink up the cabin! Blow it out the door!" Big Mama heaves herself out of her chair.

With all the air that I got in me, I blow at Randall's

bubble. I get it moving toward the door. I push the door open. The bubble floats outside of its own accord. I see the shine of Goblins. They cover their eyes to block out our light. I shout at them, "Here comes supper!"

And Big Mama shrieks at the now clearly unfroze Randall, "Don't stick that Horny Head into your mouth; it's poisoned!"

Chapter Twenty-one

Something Large and Troublesome

I don't know what I find more disturbing—the sound of Goblins fighting over the bubble I just blew outside our cabin or the sudden change that's come over Randall. It's not just that he's unfroze and no longer yellow. Nor that he's standing up to stretch so natural-like. Nor that he don't protest when Big Mama throws into the fire that Horny Head he'd been holding on to for dear life. It's that Randall just said, "Howdy," to me. Moreover, he said, "Howdy, Magpie"—not "Howdy, Skunk."

He ain't spoke so nice to me in six weeks.

I say, "Howdy, Randall. I'm glad you unfroze."

"We all are." Big Mama grabs up his right hand, which had been holding the Horny Head. She wipes the hand clean with her soapy rag. Randall regards her with a look of kind consideration in his wide dark eyes.

I haven't seen this look in Randall's eyes for quite some time. *What is going on here?* He looks over at me and says, "I had myself the strangest dream."

"Tell us about your dream." Big Mama's so grateful to have my brother unfroze that she's willing to listen to a dream.

Big Mama don't generally cotton to dreams.

"I dreamt I was inside my body," he says. "It was so dirty in there. I had an urge to clean myself up. So I got a bucket and filled it with soapy water I found in a well inside my mouth. I needed something to scrub with, so I crawled up into my nose and pulled out my nose hairs. I wove them together to form a scrubbing pad."

We glance at Randall's nose.

His nose hairs are gone.

Big Mama shoots me a look—*This is strange.*

He says, "With that pad and my bucket of soapy water, I scrubbed the black dirt off the inside of my skull. Then I went on down and scrubbed my heart. It was dirty and the scrubbing hurt. But that didn't stop me from scouring my heart clean. I went on from there to clean out my stomach, arms, hands, legs and feet. Then I took all the dirt and grit I'd scrubbed off my insides and put it inside a giant bubble. That bubble worked its way up into my throat and then out into this cabin and now, it's gone.

"I've washed myself clean. I'm hungry." Randall rubs his hands up and down his long lean stomach.

"I'll get you something to eat." Big Mama bustles off to get food for Randall but not before shooting me a second look—*See if you can figure out what's going on.*

I study my brother—once called by Big Mama the rock of our family. If something needed doing—no matter how hard or dirty it might be—Big Mama had but to ask and Randall'd do it. Randall was tough. He was strong. Nothing scared him. Like Milo's foot, Randall always had grit.

He don't look like he has grit now.

He looks scrubbed clean. Too clean.

"Randall," I say. "Tell me that even with all the scrubbing you've done, you've left a little grit inside you."

"Nope." Randall smiles. "I feel nothing but clean."

"Randall." I'm trying to be patient, but I'm nearing the end of my rope. Nothing's working out right today. "You've got to have grit somewhere inside you.

Grit's what gives you the what-all to hold on and fight for what you need."

"I told you, I ain't got grit!" Randall says.

"Well then, I just might as well go on out to Grandpa's forge and make me another link for the Sorrow Chain, because without grit, I don't see how you'll survive life in these mountains," I say.

"I'm sorry about that, Magpie," the cleaned-out Randall says.

"*Sorry?* Sorry ain't what I want to hear! I want you to say, 'I'll survive—grit or no grit. You say different and I'll crack you in the head.' And then, we'll have us a fight—like always."

"I ain't got it in me." Tears well in Randall's eyes.

Lord help us.

Grandpa's gone.

Milo's gone.

Sweet Daddy's gone.

Randall's as good as gone.

I fear Sweet Daddy's right. Something large and troublesome does have us Gabbards in its grip. What could be next? Soon as I ask myself this, I hear a ruckus going on outside the cabin. It's them Goblins. They're not fighting over that yellow bubble no more. They're whispering among themselves—

She's down, she's down,
Buried deep underground.

Who's down? Who's buried? I slip over to the window—Randall stumbling along beside me. I grab his arm to steady him. We press our ears against a pane. The whisperings grow until they sound like a thousand wild October winds assaulting our senses. An anxious Big Mama joins us.

This is what them whisperings say:

We've buried the moon.
Our reign has begun.
We'll rule each night
From dusk until dawn.

The night is now ours
After thousands of years.
We'll drink human blood
And bathe in the tears.

Chapter Twenty-two

The Sinful Maiden

ig Mama hugs Randall and me close while outside our cabin them wicked Goblins continue to carry on about burying the moon. They couldn't have buried her! For one thing, the moon's too big and powerful for anyone to do that to her. For another, it's her time of the month to rest. Right now, she's no doubt in High Jerusalem—asleep on her velvet throne.

A Goblin would never venture into High Jerusalem.

Them Goblins are lying!

When their loud uproar finally dies down, we hear them scrambling off our rooftop. A Goblin whispers at our front window:

Good, better, best,
Us Goblins never rest
'Til "good" be "better"
And "better" be "best."

The "best" is come.
The moon is gone.
We plan to party
'Til the coming of dawn.

Tell the moon good-bye.
Hi diddle hi fi!
We've brought down the moon,
And now she shall die!

And then we hear, like a giant wave of windblown leaves, them Goblins scurrying away from our cabin and down, down, down our mountainside.

And when that scurrying dies away,
and there's dead silence,
and you'd think all the Goblins in the world had left to celebrate the buried moon, I tell Big Mama and Randall, "They're trying to trick us. They want us to think they're gone. Then one of us will step outside to see if it's so and they'll suck us dry.

"As for them burying the moon—it's a lie."

"Goblins don't lie," Randall says.

"Of course they lie. Everybody lies." I'm thinking of my own part in a Bug Dirt lie.

"I don't lie," Randall says.

"You're full of lye!" I say.

"Shhhhh." Big Mama hugs us hard. "Something's working at that wall in the back room."

I now hear it, too.

SCRITCHETY—SCRATCH—SCRITCHETY—SCRATCH.

"Something's trying to get inside," Big Mama says.

"We should let it in," Randall says.

"No we shouldn't!" Big Mama and I both say.

Big Mama gives me a meaningful look—*Randall ain't right in the head.* I give her a look back—*I know.* She tells him, "We can't let it in. It's a Goblin that didn't skat and it's trying to get into our cabin.

"Magpie, go check them cow lights in the back room. Make sure they're still lit. Randall and I will stir up the fire."

I grab up one of Big Mama's cast-iron frying pans in case I need to smash some Goblin fingers. I light up a pine knot. I carry it before me into the back room, which is filled with flickering shadows. What's going on here? Them cow lights are still burning.

But them Goblin fingers scratch away anyway:

SCRITCHETY-SCRATCH.

"Cut it out!" I wham the frying pan against the wall.

Something moans—like it's trying to scare me silly.

WHAM! WHAM! WHAM! I slam the frying pan against the wall over and over again until, when I'm finally done, there is utter silence.

I fixed that left-behind Goblin good.

I light two more candles and place one on either side of the cow's skull with its burning eyes. Won't no sensible Goblin come near all that light. I go back into the front room where Big Mama, having built up the fire so it's blazing hot and bright, has started in to sing "The Sinful Maiden" while Randall eats soup.

Now, Big Mama's always been right fond of ballads dealing with poison, ill-fated love, murder, death and the ruination of women—"The Sinful Maiden" being a favorite. It concerns itself with a wayward daughter who's about to come home to her mama and daddy—hoping they'll take her in and forget the day she let some n'er-do-well out of jail and into her heart, which got her into trouble.

When Big Mama sings this ballad, it's most always aimed at me. Tonight, Big Mama aims her voice at

Randall. I reckon she wants the newly washed and gritless Randall to realize this world ain't all sweetness and light. There's n'er-do-wells out there. Beware.

Big Mama sings the ballad straight through. She must be just getting up her steam, for when she's done, she starts in again:

> As she walked by the jailhouse,
> The maiden heard a fellow say:
> "It's growing cold and lonesome here,
> Help me to get away."

And there comes a rap-rap-rapping from the back room.

"That's the lonesome fellow!" Randall puts aside his soup and rises. "He's cold! I'll let him in!"

"Oh no you won't! It could be a n'er-do-well—the Goblin!" Big Mama forces Randall to sit down. She grabs up the Chain of Sorrows from where I'd left it—thrown next to the woodpile. I help her to quickly wrap the chain around Randall—chaining his arms against his body and his body to the chair so he can't go and do something foolish.

Randall don't protest. He just sits there saying, "The poor fellow. We need to let him in."

Big Mama and I get Randall so chained up, he can't move.

First Milo was in chains.

Then it was me.

Now Randall.

The rapping turns to pounding.

In the back room, Big Mama and I set a flaming pine knot in a large frying pan. We set that pan with the burning pine knot on top of a grinding stone. We set that stone on top of a barrel alongside the table holding the cow's skull and four flaming candles.

Once we get the room bright as we possibly can, the pounding stops. But every time I go in there to make certain them lights are still burning, I hear something breathing right outside the wall.

I scream at it—over and over—"Go away."

But it don't.

Chapter Twenty-three

Rising to the Occasion

Up in the loft, our rooster announces, "Daylight's here." The chickens flutter down the stairs. The livestock in the Hidey-Hole start in to talking among themselves. The babble of sheep, cows, hogs and Sweet Daddy's mule, Old Blue, comes up through the floorboards—*It's time to go outside.*

We can't let any creature out until we know what's breathing outside the back room. Is it a crazed Goblin who don't know better than to flee the sun's light?

Or is it something else?

"Be careful, Magpie." Big Mama hands me her hog rifle.

"Don't shoot the lonesome fellow!" Randall, still

chained to his chair, grips the seat bottom and hops, chair and all, toward me. He shouts, "Don't shoot! Don't shoot."

"Randall! Hush up!" Big Mama clamps down on his chair so he can't move. To me she says, "You go on. Holler if you need me."

I step out of the cabin and into daylight. The daylight this morning feels strange. Not at all like yesterday with its intense sunshine. Today it feels like the sun has come down sick with a cold and it don't feel up to shining like it should. Stranger still, there's no birdsong; we always have birdsong come morning. There's no wind either.

All's quiet.

Too quiet.

What's going on now?

I edge around the north side of the cabin with rifle in hand. I watch where I put my feet. I don't want to step on something I shouldn't—a half-dead Goblin or a twig that might startle that Goblin awake. I prepare myself for the worst. I tell myself, "Magpie, you can handle anything."

But even saying this don't prepare me for what I now see.

It's no half-dead Goblin.

It's my own Sweet Daddy.

He's curled on the ground with his back sheltered against the outside wall of the back room and a shivering dog on either side of him. All night long, it must have been my own Sweet Daddy, scratching, rapping, pounding and then sighing outside that back room—begging us to let him in.

And we didn't.

If only his dogs had barked! Why didn't they bark? Did Goblins scare that bark clean out of them? Tears in my eyes, I throw myself on the ground beside Sweet Daddy. His dogs rise and lick at my tears, but Sweet Daddy don't move. He don't look right. He looks as withered as a sun-dried grape. I see—right where his mud-stained coat collar grazes his neck—two spots of blood.

A Goblin bit him. But it didn't suck him dry. If it had, Sweet Daddy wouldn't be here now. Something must have frightened off the Goblin in midbite. I touch Sweet Daddy's cheek. He whimpers. He covers his head with his hands.

"Sweet Daddy—I'm your own sweet Magpie—come to help you inside." I put my hand under his arm. His dogs whine as I help Sweet Daddy to his feet. He shivers like an old man with the palsy.

"We got a warm fire burning in the front room." I need that fire myself. I'm shivering. He puts a withered hand on my arm for support, but he don't say a word. I glance sideways at his face. His eyes are blank and staring.

He allows me to lead him around the cabin and through the front door. Soon as Big Mama sees him, she wails, "I told myself he was safe at Doc's!"

Big Mama lifts Sweet Daddy up in her strong arms. Cradling Sweet Daddy like he was her baby, Big Mama carries him over to their bed in the back room while I follow and Randall hops after us in his chair.

"What happened to Sweet Daddy?" Randall says.

"He'd gone to Squabble Town to get Green Water for you and a Goblin bit him." I sniff up my tears. Now ain't the time for crying. I got to buckle up and be strong.

"Why'd I need Green Water?" Randall says.

"To heal you," I say.

"I'm already healed!" Randall says.

"Oh no you ain't," I say. "You're too nice. If a poison snake was to shake its rattle at you, you'd pet it."

"I reckon I would," he says.

We watch Big Mama lay Sweet Daddy gently down. She plumps the pillow beneath his head. He turns to stare blank eyed at the window where the cow's skull still sits, its candles burned to nubs. His dogs crawl beneath the bed and settle there.

"It's a miracle he's alive." Big Mama rubs Sweet Daddy's hands. "You find any Green Water on him?"

"He didn't have none," I say.

"No Green Water?" Tears sparkle her eyes. "Doc must have been out of it. Otherwise, your Sweet Daddy would have brought it home—one way or another. If we had Green Water, we could dose Randall with it and your Sweet Daddy, too. That miracle water would cure them both.

"What do we do now, Magpie?" She turns her tear-filled eyes on me. This is the first time in my life that Big Mama has asked me what to do. She should know what to do—not me. All I wanted was to return a foot.

And now Big Mama's got tears,
and Randall ain't right in the head,
and neither is Sweet Daddy,
and I'm all that she's got left.
I don't have no choice but to rise to the occasion.
"I'll find us Green Water," I say.
"Where will you find it?" Big Mama says.
"I'll go see Granny. I'll ask her to consult about it

with her prophesying kettle. That kettle should know." Without waiting for Big Mama to fully consider what I'm about to do (finding this Green Water will no doubt mean I'll have to leave our mountain), I run out the door. In the front room, I grab up Milo's foot and slip it back into my apron pocket.

Some folks carry a rabbit's foot for luck.

I'll carry Milo's.

If luck prevails, I'll come upon him in my journey.

Chapter Twenty-four

Granny's Prophesying Kettle

ranny's shed backs up against a rocky slope that leads to the highest spot on our mountain. We got boulders up there with Cherokee Indian drawings of the moon in all her phases on them. Them boulders are placed just so and if you position yourself between the largest of them, you can be first on our mountain to watch the moon rise above the distant mountain ridges before taking her place high in our sky.

Milo and I liked to go to that high spot on clear nights. We'd stand together and as the moon rose, Milo would play a tune for her on his hands. He called it "The Moonshine Song." The moon seemed to rise more glorious on account of that song. I imagined her smile each time Milo played it.

But all the times I went to that high spot with Milo, we'd always hurry by Granny Goforth's consultation shed with its crooked stone chimney and prophesying kettle. We never once stepped inside it together, him and me. For one thing, Granny never invited us in. For another, she's got a sign nailed to the fir tree against which she's propped her firewood. That sign says, *You Keep Out, You Hear?* For a third, Granny don't have no teeth and when she'd smile, the sight of her toothless mouth would scare us silly.

I now climb Granny's two front steps.

I hammer on Granny's pinewood door— knockety-knock.

"Who's there?" Granny screeches.

"It's me, Magpie," I holler.

One of Granny's large rheumy eyes looks out at me through a knothole in the door.

"It's me, I swear."

"No need for swearing." Granny's door opens and as I'm saying, "Howdy, Granny," she's pulling me into the consultation shed and slamming shut the door. Everything's dark in here and smoke-blackened to boot, so I can't even make out Granny's toothless grin. If Granny had eaten Grandpa's honey like the rest of us, she'd still have a grin of pure white teeth.

ut, as Granny's often said, she don't like honey and she never will.

She don't ask why I've come to see her. She just drags me around a table and chair and over to her steaming black prophesying kettle, hanging in the fireplace, bright flames licking at its bottom. The one time I looked into this kettle, I saw Milo.

Granny says, "Look inside the kettle and tell me what you see."

"I see steam." It covers the kettle like a cloud.

Granny waves her hand across the kettle water. The steam clears. What I see now is so horrifying I can't speak. I see a woman. She's buried beneath layers of tree branches in a deep and watery bog hole. Writhing vines have bound her hands together. Her long black robe whips through the water as she struggles to escape.

All of a sudden, the woman stops struggling.

All of a sudden, she looks up at me.

All of a sudden, her face shines forth at me so soft and kind with golden hair streaming out around it. I know that shining. I've seen it in the sky. She mouths the words, "Magpie, help me."

"I'm seeing the moon!" I tell Granny. All my life, I've heard of her coming to earth as a woman. I've never seen her myself, but Sweet Daddy has. "The B Goblins did this. Last night, I heard them crowing about burying her . . . I didn't believe them."

"You know the prophecy," Granny says.

"One day I'm to save us all—including the moon." I ain't ready to fulfill this prophecy! As much as I'd like to, I can't. I'm only thirteen. And there's Milo to save, and Sweet Daddy, and Randall, too.

Granny grabs my arm. While holding tight to me, she shrieks, "Kettle, show Magpie how she's to save the moon." Granny sweeps her free arm across the kettle water. It steams up something fierce. When it clears I don't see the moon no more. I see a pond of bright green water. Is this the one and only Green Water Pond where Doc gets his miracle cure? I bet it is.

A girl with red hair sits on the pond's bank with her arms wrapped around her knees. An old granny woman sits on one side of her. A white-haired boy and a funny-looking cat with ears that turn down at the tips sit on the other.

"Why's the kettle showing me this?" I ask.

"That girl can tell you what you need to do to bring the moon back to our sky," Granny says.

"How do you know that?" I say.

"Watch this! I've done it several times. I always get the same answer.

"Kettle! Does the Red-Haired Girl know how Magpie can save the moon?" Granny sweeps her arm across the kettle water. It steams up once more. It puffs three steamy letters out into the air—one after the other—

Y - - - - - E - - - - - S

Then it goes back to the green pond scene.

If that's Doc's Green Pond, I could get me two birds with one stone. I could get Green Water and find out how to save the moon as well!

The Red-Haired Girl lifts her head. She's got green eyes the color of the pond. Them eyes lock themselves on mine. The girl jumps to her feet. She yells at the granny woman and the white-haired boy while pointing upward and at me.

"That girl sees me through this kettle water!" *The same way the moon did. This must be a girl with power.*

"You need to go to that girl, Magpie. She's far away—over the state line and into the Tennessee mountains. Traveling by foot, it'll take you several weeks to reach her. But I've discovered in my consultations a key for getting to her fast."

Wild Bill's the only creature I know that can get anyplace fast. I hope this key don't involve him. I don't have sparkles for dealing with him.

"Kettle! Show us who holds the key!" Granny sweeps her arm across the kettle. When the steam clears, I nearly faint, for I see a silver key—lying on the large pink tongue inside the open mouth of a man's hairy bearded head floating in an old stone well.

"Granny! Is that the Floating Head I've heard about since I was knee-high to a goose?" I shriek. "The Head of that evil man who killed my great-great-grandfather?"

Granny says, "It is."

Chapter Twenty-five

Great-Grandmother Margaret's Curse

Long ago, before Goblins tailed my Great-Grandmother Margaret across the sea and here to Kentucky, that Head didn't float in an old stone well—at the northeast entrance to the Cob Hollow Path. That Head was stuck on a pike at a market gate in England. Every day, Great-Grandmother Margaret would pass by that Head on her way to market. Every day that Head cried out to her—"I didn't kill your daddy!"

Great-Grandmother grew tired of hearing the Head protest its innocence. Of course it had killed her daddy. Hadn't the court found it guilty of that very deed? So on the day she turned thirteen, Great-Grandmother used her magic sparkles to curse the Head. She went right up to it and spat—"A pox on you!" The Head was immediately covered in boils.

This didn't stop it from calling out to Great-Grandmother whenever she walked by. But now, instead of saying it didn't kill her daddy, the Head just cried, "Take pity's sake on me. Remove this curse."

Great-Grandmother never did.

It's said that when them Goblins followed Great-Grandmother to Kentucky, they brought the Head with them. It must have been a hard journey for the Head. The first time it was seen here, not only was it cursed with boils, but its beard and hair had become dirty and tangled and covered in burrs. Now it cries out to all who pass by—"For pity's sake, comb out my beard and hair."

"That Head's been hollering for someone to comb it out for nigh onto a hundred years," Granny tells me now. "You oblige the Head by doing it and I reckon the Head will give you the key for getting fast to the Red-Haired Girl."

There's got to be an easier way to get that key than combing out a Head, but I don't tell Granny that. I just pocket the comb she hands me while saying, "Is that pond I'll be heading for the one and only miracle pond where Doc Buckle gets Green Water?"

Granny says, "There's no pond that green anyplace around here, so I reckon it is."

Good. That clinches it. I'll get Green Water. I'll

talk to the girl. Maybe I'll come upon Milo on the way and give him back his foot. Maybe this is the way it's all meant to be. Who'd have thought it would be so easy?

I'm ready to go back to bed!

I tell Granny about Randall and Sweet Daddy.

"Big Mama will need help with them while I'm gone," I say.

"She'll get that help." Granny eyeballs me. I reckon now she's gonna launch into me about the Bug Dirt. She must have seen, in her kettle, my handing Thelma Bug Dirt with a smile. I brace myself but Granny don't say nothing about it. Instead, she gives me things for what she calls "the hard journey ahead." Besides a comb, I get:

1. A flask to fill with the Green Water that will save lives.

2. A gourd full of Grandpa's honey that Granny's been saving for a time like this. She says, "You're to use it for placating Sizemores. You might come across Sizemores on your way to the Head. The well it's in is on Sizemore property.

"You know how to tell a Sizemore from a Gabbard," she says.

I answer, "By our teeth." Us folks on Gabbard

Mountain all have snow-white teeth on account of eating Grandpa's honey except, of course, for Granny, who don't have any teeth at all. Them Sizemores' teeth are brown. That's from drinking creosote. You'd think it would kill them, but it don't. I'm told creosote's the only drink strong enough to satisfy their craving for our honey.

I ain't placating no thieving Sizemore with Grandpa's honey!

3. Directions. I'm to head out from Granny's—taking the shortcut over the highest spot on our mountain. I'm to hurry down the rocky path that follows the course of Cheerful Creek. At the bottom of the mountain, I'm to turn left onto Squabble Town Road. I'll pass Sizemore apple orchards. I'm not to pick Sizemore apples. Granny says, "Magpie, let sleeping dogs lie." I'm to follow the road to where it curves sharply right—at which point, I'm to go straight and onto the rugged-looking *Cob Hollow Path*.

From there, I'm to follow my ears.

My ears will lead me to the Head.

I am not to tarry.

"You ain't got time." Granny leans into my face. "You ain't got but thirteen days. According to my kettle, if you don't free the moon between now and the time she should be waxing full—October sixteenth—she'll never rise again. The earth will fall into dark decay. Them wicked Cob Hollow Goblins will take over the night. What they don't eat, they'll turn into one of their own kind and soon, all of life as we know it—except for them Goblins—will die."

"Then I'd better hurry," I say.

Chapter Twenty-six

Here I Come

I t don't take me long to figure out that the moon and Milo have the same deadline—October 16th. I don't know what deadline Randall and Sweet Daddy might have, but I reckon the sooner I get Green Water to them, the better.

It all comes down to me. I've got the world to save in thirteen days. You'd think with the weight of this resting on my shoulders, I'd have fire in my belly and wings on my feet. Well, I don't. I'm tired. I've been stumbling over rocks and making my way down-mountain for over two hours. I haven't reached the bottom yet.

It don't help that Cheerful Creek, named for the happy sound its water makes as it courses downhill, ain't running cheerful today. It runs as sluggish as I feel. If that creek weren't heading downhill, I reckon

108

it wouldn't run at all. And no wonder. It don't have the moon's glowing fingertips to pull it along. Everyone knows her fingertips pull all the waters on this earth—causing them to ebb and flow and sing and dance all a-sparkle and glad to be alive.

A pale sun shines through trees with sad leaves drooping. Their colors are faded like old cloth dried too long in the sun. No wind blows to perk them up. I ain't heard a bird chirp, nor squirrel chide me. Without the moon, the world ain't got no get-up-and-go.

Neither do I.

If only this were yesterday. Then, I had sparkles. I could have used them sparkles to get Green Water, save the moon, save Milo and the rest of my family, too. How am I ever gonna save anyone the way I feel now, as tired as Cheerful Creek and cranky to boot?

To wake myself up, I kick at stones with my bare feet. I pound my sides. I holler to a countryside I ain't never seen before—"I'm Margaret Magpie Gabbard! Here I come!" It keeps me going. Finally, I reach the bottom of our mountain. Here, where Cheerful Creek veers off to the right, I turn left onto the Squabble Town Road—a rutted wagon road full of potholes.

You'd think I'd be nervous—leaving Gabbard Mountain for the first time in my life. I'm too worn-out to feel nervous. I kick my feet along the dusty road. I sing "The Sinful Maiden" to keep myself awake. My singing startles a turkey buzzard. The large bird tumbles off the branch of a nearby apple tree and onto the ground. It lifts its red head and it hisses at me. It flaps up and onto the branch of a second apple tree. It teeters—holding on to the branch for dear life.

This turkey buzzard is the first live creature I've seen since I left Granny Goforth. And even though a buzzard's a sure sign of something dead or nearly dead, still, I whoop for joy. I ain't alone in this sorry world. But when I catch sight of the animal hide stuck to the tree where the buzzard's alighted, my whoop dies.

That hide's got words painted on it.

Them words read:

Sizemore Propertee—You Gabbards Keep Out.

I spit at the hide. I nail it good—several times. Then I, Margaret Magpie Gabbard, keeper of the Gabbard flame of ire and downright indignation against them pernicious Sizemores, step my Gabbard foot on Sizemore Propertee. That lifts my spirits. Thrusting my chin up and out, I throw back my shoulders. I trudge ever onward toward the Floating Head—the turkey buzzard now soaring above me on wide, dark, silver-lined wings.

Chapter Twenty-seven

The Head

At the sharp turn in the Squabble Town Road where I'm to leave the road and head straight onto the Cob Hollow Path, the turkey buzzard banks. I watch it follow the course of the road that, I'm told, curves like a corkscrew for another three miles before reaching town. Whoever built the road didn't want to run it through Cob Hollow even though that's a shortcut to town and can get you there in half the time.

Telling myself that many Gabbards have taken the Cob Hollow Path and come out alive, I step off the road and onto the narrow footpath. Soon as I do, a thin, high voice wails—"Won't someone take pity's sake on me?"

The Head.

Well, at least I don't have to be traipsing this way and that trying to find *the Head.*

"I'm heading into rack and ruin!" the Head cries out. It sure talks funny. But I reckon it would—being from England. I follow its caterwauling off the path and through a tangled mass of mountain laurel. On the other side, in the center of a small clearing, stands an open-sided well house—its wood roof full of holes. I step up and into the little house. A few feet below me, a hatless, hairy, bearded head bobs like an apple on top of the water in a circular pool no more than three feet wide.

Great-Grandmother Margaret did a fine job of cursing this Head. It's been over a hundred years since she cried out, "A pox on you," and still, boils cover its reddened forehead, cheeks and nose. It's the ugliest head I ever saw—all boils, red skin and burrs matting its dirty beard and hair.

"Take pity's sake on me! Comb me out," the Head whines up at me.

I catch the twinkle of silver in its mouth.

The key for getting to the Green Pond fast.

I settle myself at the well's edge and dangle my hand in the water—trying to look casual. *I need to get that key.* I tell the Head, "You keep whining, you'll waste your voice away."

"I only call when I hear someone coming," the Head says. "I can't *see* the path from inside this well, but, if I hold my head just so, I can *hear* quite well.

"Not if I hold my head this way, mind you." The Head flings itself backward so it's floating on its burred and tangled mass of hair with its two brown eyes staring up at me and its two large ears completely underwater.

"Nor this way." It flings itself face forward and blows bubbles.

"But this way." It fixes itself so it's bobbing upright once again. "And do you know what I just saw in my most recent perambulations? I saw that you have the most remarkable hair."

"I was born with this hair," I say.

"You were?" The Head rolls its eyes at me. Does it recall my Great-Grandmother Margaret's black and white hair?

I quickly add, "All sorts of folks have hair like mine." This is a lie. I'm the only one I know of.

"I used to have a handsome head of hair," it says. "I still could—if someone would comb it out."

I don't say nothing to that.

There ain't no way I'm combing out this Head!

"In the Old Country, I sold hair by the sackful," the Head continues. "I'd be selling hair still if Tom

Cobbley hadn't borrowed Bess—my gray mare—to go across the windswept moors and over to the Fair."

Tom Cobbley was my great-great-grandfather.

"But you don't want to hear about all this." The Head rolls its eyes like it's begging me to disagree.

"Of course I want to hear." That'll give me time to figure out how to get that key. But I got to do it fast. I only got thirteen days to get Milo out of Purgatory and the moon out of that bog hole. God alone knows how long I got to bring Sweet Daddy and Randall out of their sorrowful states.

"Well, I warned Tom—be back with Bess from that Fair before nightfall," the Head goes on. "But he didn't listen. And he never returned—although Bess and my wagon did. Word leaked out that I'd killed him. And for what, I ask you? Why would I, Tam Pierce, kill Tom Cobbley?" The Head flips backward so it can look at me once more.

"I reckon you might have killed him for his hair." *And you ain't getting mine. I ain't trading you my hair for your key.*

How can I get that key?

"I did not kill him!" Tam glares at me.

I back off a little.

"Being decapitated for a crime I didn't commit was a travesty! But it wasn't as bad as you might think." He grins—baring two sets of yellow teeth. I see, once more, between them, the gleam of silver. "For I was stuck on a pike at the entrance to the market. Here Bess and my most stalwart of friends—Sir William, whom I raised since birth—could visit me daily.

"Sir William's royalty, you know. He comes from the noblest stock and can carry on the most civilized conversations. But then, one dark night, Goblins came out of the moors and stole me away—for a lark!" Tam rolls his eyes at me to make sure I'm listening.

"Go on." If I listen long enough, maybe he'll just give me the key.

"They stuffed me in a sack and smuggled me on board a ship bound for America. Me—prone to seasickness! When the ship finally docked and I thought I'd be settled on a nice pike by the sea, those Goblins headed inland with me.

"Now, as you no doubt have already ascertained, I'm not the kind of Head to remain quiet about things. I protested their rough treatment! But should I be punished for speaking up?" Tam rolls his eyes in my direction once more.

I reckon this is a trick question—a kind of test for me. I say, "Of course not."

"OF COURSE NOT," Tam agrees. "It's quite normal to speak up! When your head's chopped off you shout—'This is a travesty!' When Pilgrims stop to talk, you say, 'Hello, good friends!' And when you're uprooted from the home you love and stuck in a sack for days and jostled this way and that, you have a right to protest—'This torture is unspeakable!'

"The Goblins did not take this kindly. When they finally removed me from that filthy sack, they swung me by my hair through a cocklebur patch. Burrs in my beard! Burrs in my hair! Then they threw me in this well, where I've been floating ever since.

"It can be a lonely well—even though Bess and my good friend Sir William smuggled themselves on board ship and followed me here. Those cruel Goblins put a sleeping spell on Bess. They buried her—not far from here. As for Sir William, he's too fast for those Goblins to catch. He's grown quite wild—roaming this Kentucky soil. However, he does visit me weekly for 'a civilizing talk to.' I hold the key to his heart, you see."

Tam opens his mouth so that I can see that key.

He says, "And now, dear Pilgrim, for I see that's

what you are—a searcher of what's good and holy. You're the first to ever pause and listen to my story since I reached these shores. Pray, tell me, what may I do for you?"

Finally.

I say, "I reckon you could give me that key."

Chapter Twenty-eight

A Hog by Any Other Name Is Still a Hog

ow on Gabbard Mountain, it's tit for tat. You do something nice for someone—like listening to their life's story. And then they ask, "What can I do for you in return?" And you tell them. You expect them to do it for you right away. You don't expect them to be hemming and hawing the way Tam's doing right now. Saying he can't give up the key to Sir William's heart. "How can I?" Tam says. "When Sir William arrived here in Kentucky, he gave me the key for safekeeping.

"As long as I hold the key, Sir William knows he can't run so completely wild, he'll lose all sense of British propriety. He'll always come back to me for a civilizing conversation and a brushup on his manners.

"Ask anything else of me, Pilgrim. Anything!" Tam says.

Well, I can't! Even though I don't know what this Sir William is or how the key to his heart will help me get to the Green Pond fast—STILL I KNOW I NEED THAT KEY.

Granny and her kettle said so.

Once I get the key, I'll go from there.

I study them ugly-looking boils Tam's got and the prickly cockleburs matting his beard and hair and a BRIGHT IDEA comes to me. Now I ain't generally known for BRIGHT IDEAS. Milo's always been the one for that. But I reckon when you're on your own, you rise to the occasion.

I take out Granny's comb. I run it through my black and white hair. Tam watches me. I don't say nothing. I just comb through my smooth, flowing burr-free hair.

"If I were to give you the key to Sir William's heart, would you comb out my hair, too?" Tam says.

"I don't think all the combing in the world would fix your hair," I say. "But Green Water would. You ever heard of Green Water? If I had it, I'd put it on this comb. Them burrs and tangles would ease right out. Green Water would also clear up them boils you got. Only to get this miracle cure, I'd have to travel to the only place it can be found—faraway Eastern Tennessee. If you'd give me the key to Sir

William's heart, I could get there fast." There, I've said it all.

"If I gave you the key, how can I be sure you'd return with it and then, take care of me?" Tam says.

"Don't a Pilgrim always keep her word?" I ain't no Pilgrim. Never said I was.

I ain't about to comb out this Head.

"Take the key!" Tam sticks out his tongue. I grab up the key and wipe it off with my apron.

"Now, Tam. A key's good for nothing unless you know how to use it."

"You don't know?" Tam says.

"I'd hoped by holding it, I'd know, but I don't," I say.

"It's a winding key, Pilgrim. With it, you wind up Sir William's heart and he'll take you wherever you need to go. One moment you're *here.* Moments later, he's carried you *elsewhere.*"

Wild Bill's the only creature I know that can carry you someplace fast. I hope this Sir William's nothing like him.

"But there's something you must know," Tam says. "The journey elsewhere feels like it lasts only moments—in truth, alas, it takes three days. Wherever Sir William takes you—even if it's to the market down the street—it will take three days. He has to travel through WHITE SPACE, you see."

Three days? That don't sound fast. But on foot and on my own, I might never make it to them Tennessee mountains. I do some calculating in my head. Getting to the Green Pond—that's three days there. Coming home—that's another three. That makes six days. Thirteen minus six is seven.

I'll still have seven days to save everyone—provided Randall and Sweet Daddy can last that long.

"How do I wind up Sir William?" I ask Tam. I'm biding my time to ask who Sir William is—and where?

"Insert the silver key into the small hole just behind where his left foreleg joins his body. Push the key until you feel his heart clamp onto it. Then wind the key slowly until you hear a loud click. Never wind beyond the click!"

This sounds mighty strange.

"Once he's wound, you may climb on board. Hold on to his ears—gently, mind you—and shout into them for all you're worth exactly where you need to go. Pepper your directions with details that will be alluring to him—such as oak trees laden with acorns and soft grassy vistas and cool mud. It's all in the details, Pilgrim."

Acorns? Grassy vistas? Mud?

"When you have your Green Water, shout, 'Sir William, take me to my old friend Tam!' And Sir William will.

"Always keep his key somewhere on you. Never give it to Sir William himself! If you should, he'll turn completely wild. I'll never see him again.

"Finally and foremost, do not ride Sir William every which way and that. For each time he carries you through WHITE SPACE, it weakens him. He could fade away! And where would I be then? I'd be a Head without his hog!"

"Did you just say hog?" I scream.

Chapter Twenty-nine

Sir William Meets Pilgrim

T am did say hog because that's what Sir
William is. Then Tam called that hog. I'm
seated on that hog right now. Only I'd never
call him a hog. I'd call him a wild Kentucky boar—the
selfsame boar I rode yesterday when I had my
sparkles—Wild Bill!

Who'd have thought Wild Bill would have come
from England?

And from noble stock?

He'll always be Wild Bill to me. I got him wound
up and ready to go. He's acting real nice now that I
hold the key to his heart. When Tam introduced us—
"Sir William, meet Pilgrim"—Wild Bill nodded his
head and grunted, just like he was saying, "Delighted
to meet you." He acted as if he'd never seen me be-

fore nor knocked me teacup over kettle. However, as I was winding him up, I did feel his nose pushing at the gourd of honey Granny strapped to my side.

Wild Bill and Tam say their fare-thee-wells by rubbing noses. I tell you, these two are a pair—an ugly Head and a conniving boar. Who'd have thought Wild Bill would have a heart with a windup key? Or that he'd love a Head so much, he followed him here from England?

Life is peculiar.

Tam says to me, "Take care of Sir William. Make sure he gets plenty to eat. Don't overtire him. And don't be frightened by the WHITE SPACE he'll take you through to reach that healing Green Water Pond. I find it helps to say IMPORTANT WORDS while going through WHITE SPACE.

"For example, if it were me mounted on Sir William, I'd say to myself over and over, 'Tam, hold on to your head!' "

"I'll remember that," I say.

"Come back soon, Pilgrim."

Pilgrim. I'm beginning to like that name. Maybe I am a Pilgrim. I'm searching for something good and holy—a way to save the moon. I grab hold of Wild Bill's hairy ears. Today, instead of shouting into them,

"Wild Bill, take me to Milo," I shout for all I'm worth, "Wild Bill, take me to the Green Pond. It's got cool sweet mud for you to wallow in and fulsome oak trees full of delicious acorns for you to eat."

Wild Bill backs up from the well. He pushes through the laurel patch with me on board and Tam calling out, "Pilgrim! His name's Sir William."

Not in my book.

Wild Bill turns onto the Cob Hollow Path and trots back toward the Squabble Town Road. This time he don't buck, nor try to throw me off, but his rough gait does jar my bones. I hang on as best I can. The distant sky above the trees appears to pulse with flashes of what looks like sheet lightning.

At the road, I remind Wild Bill of where we need to go and he breaks into a bone-cracking run. He picks up speed—running ever faster. A dank wind whips through my night-sky hair. I see the faded colored blur of October leaves and then, Wild Bill lifts off the ground and there ain't no colored blur no more.

There ain't nothing but WHITE SPACE.

It sucks at my hair.

IT WANTS TO SUCK ME UP!

"Margaret Magpie Gabbard! Hold on to your head!" I shriek.

125

Chapter Thirty

The Age-Old Prophecy

The next thing I know, I'm tumbling off Wild Bill's back. I land, bottoms down, on the bank of the greenest pond I've ever seen. The Red-Haired Girl I saw in Granny's kettle runs along the bank toward me. Did she see me coming on Wild Bill? I'm glad I didn't have to search for her. I could get lost in these Tennessee mountains. The girl's about my size but older looking in a pink flowered dress and with her red hair flying free.

I jump to my feet—startling Wild Bill. He trots off toward a nearby clutch of oak trees. I turn to the girl. She's got the greenest eyes. She fixes them eyes on me and I feel like a bug caught in lantern light. Pumping my hand, she says, "Howdy. You took your time getting here."

"It's the boar's fault—not mine. It takes him three days to carry me anywhere." We stare at that boar. Head now lowered, he roots for acorns.

"We got a heap to talk about. Have yourself a seat." The girl lowers herself to the pond bank. I settle beside her. I notice for the first time that the edges of the pond ain't as bright green as they were when I saw them in Granny's kettle.

Is this on account of the moon's being buried?

It's been three days.

She says, "You need to know I got the second sight, which means I see and sense things others can't. For instance, I knew you was coming. Your imminent arrival set my hair roots tingling. I also know the moon's in trouble and you've come to me to find out how to save her."

"That's right." This is the most up-front and knowing girl I've ever met. Course I've only ever known but one other girl in my lifetime—Thelma.

This girl says, "I'd be lying if I told you I didn't want to be the one to save the moon. I got a strong need to be a hero. Always have. But however much I want to do it, I also know you have to be the one. You, with that crescent moon streaking through your night-dark hair.

"What's your name?" she says.

I tell her.

She says, "Magpie Gabbard, you have your work cut out for you." She grabs hold of my two hands. I let her hold on to them. *I have my work cut out for me.*

She says, "With my mind's eye, I saw Goblins roll a giant stone on top of the buried moon. I saw them dance around that stone. Their king raised his hands above his crown of bones. He cast a spell—binding stone to earth. It was a terrifying sight."

"Where is this stone?" I'll lift it up and free the moon.

That moon's been struggling for three days.

"You'll find the stone in a dark, steep-sided hollow—filled with marl pits, bog holes, dead leaves and Goblin lairs. It's got a swinging bridge at one end, leading to a town," she says.

"Why, that's Cob Hollow! It's near where I live," I shriek.

"The moon's buried there." The girl's eyes bare into mine. "But you can't break the Goblin King's spell and lift the stone all on your own. You'll need twenty-six people—young, old, male and female—to help you."

128

"*Twenty-six?* I can't come up with that many."
We only have thirteen on our mountain and then,
there's Milo, and, now, of course, there's Tam, but he's
only a Head.

She says, "You must! You have to! It says so in
THE AGE-OLD PROPHECY. It's been passed down
through these mountains for years. Listen to what it
says. Listen hard." Her green eyes grow cloudy, like
she's now tapping into that prophecy for herself.

"Thirteen of these twenty-six folks must have
brown teeth," she intones. "Twelve of the others must
have teeth white as driven snow and then there's the
thirteenth and she ain't got no teeth at all."

I know what she's describing. She's describing
them low-down Sizemores and us upright Gabbard
Mountain folk—all coming together as one.

I withdraw my hands from hers.

She don't seem to notice.

She says, "At dusk, either on or before the night
the moon's supposed to wax full, the GAL WITH
THE BLACK AND WHITE HAIR—that's you, Magpie—
must lead all these folk down, down, down into
that hollow.

"It will be a dangerous undertaking," she says.

She has no idea how dangerous. Them Sizemores

don't have a speck of good in them. Not a speck! They'll start fistfights. There'll be shoot-outs.

She says, "Fear nothing! Do exactly as I say. Move out into the hollow. Them Goblins will harass you. Don't pay them any mind. They can't hurt you in the twilight—only after dark descends.

"Don't carry torchlight. Light will befuddle you. Don't say a word unless you have to. Look right. You got to look right to find the moon. You do that and all of a sudden-like you'll see a low-lying swamp lit by a Goblin's blue lantern hanging from a dead tree shaped like a cross. Beneath this lantern stands the giant stone holding down the moon.

"Make everyone join hands in a circle around the stone—brown tooth holding on to white tooth and clear around to the one with no teeth at all."

Sizemores and Gabbards holding hands?

She says, "Circle the stone three times in one direction and three times in the other. As you all do, say aloud the following words over and over again:

> *God bless you,*
> *God bless me,*
> *God bless the moon that we set free.*

"Doing this will break the Goblin King's binding spell so that you can, all together, lift the giant stone and free the moon." For the first time, she smiles at me. She says, "That's all you have to do, Magpie."

That's all.

Well, this is one impossible moon-saving plan!

Chapter Thirty-one

The Power of Love

I'm mounted on Wild Bill once more. He ain't happy about it. He sagged when I got on. And here I'd given him time to eat acorns on top of which I just fed him a generous handful of honey. I figured it was only fair. I need Wild Bill to carry me further and longer than I'd first planned and I can't have him fading out on me.

The Red-Haired Girl hands me my flask, which she's kindly filled with Green Water. I told her about the sad state of my family—the ones with the snow-white teeth who, she says, have to join forces with the brown teeth. She said, "Green Water will heal them. It's powered by love. There ain't nothing more powerful than that. Love's the glue that binds us all together.

"You'll need love in your heart to save the moon," she says.

I'll need a whole lot more than that.

"Wish I could come along with you, Magpie. Maybe, one day, you and I could join forces."

She looks as if she'd like this and, having no grudge against her besides her passing on to me a saving plan I can't stomach, I say, "Maybe we will."

Now you might expect at this point, I'd be shouting into Wild Bill's hairy ears, "Wild Bill! Take me to where them Sizemores live," while doing my best to add details that would be attractive to him.

You'd be dead wrong.

Before doing that, I'd die.

I'm finally going to see Milo. Because before all this mess started, that's where I was off to. If there's one thing I've learned it's this—before you save anyone, you have to save yourself. By seeing Milo, I'll do just that. For Milo's always been the one for BRIGHT IDEAS. When he grew too breathless to sing, he made trumpet music with his hands. He invented cow skull lights. He designed our water system. He's bound to know a better way to save the moon than having to hobnob with the enemy.

And I'll give him back his foot.

So I shout into Wild Bill's awaiting ears, "Take me to Milo's sycamore in Purgatory, Kentucky. There'll be tasty nuts for you to eat, a clear and flowing stream to drink from and shade in which to take a well-earned nap."

Wild Bill trots right out. I hold on to my head. The last I see of the Red-Haired Girl are her intense green eyes and her waving good-bye hand. I never did catch her name.

Chapter Thirty-two

Ghost Dog

The problem with riding Wild Bill is that you have to give him detailed travel directions that are appealing to his taste. And so I'd told the boar to take me to Milo's sycamore in Purgatory, where there'd be nuts, a stream and shade. I said nothing about taking me to Milo himself.

This was one big mistake.

Milo's not at his sycamore tree!

HE AIN'T HERE!

I've called and called him. I've searched all up and down this narrow valley. No Milo—although I did find signs of him and Talker inside the hollowed-out tree trunk Milo's turned into a home—a dog's water dish, a cup of cold spicewood tea, some firewood and, most important and troubling for me, a pile of half-carved wooden feet.

Milo's been trying to make himself a foot.

And here, I've got the real one with me.

Where is he?

If I could, I'd mount Wild Bill again. I'd holler at him, "Take me to Milo. He loves all animals. He'll give you a head scratch and an ear rub, too." But that wouldn't be fair to Wild Bill. After six days of travel, he's plumb worn-out. He sprawls among curls of whitened bark that Milo's sycamore has shed. Leaves—faded to dead brown—hang from tree branches overhead. I don't hear any birds or scolding squirrels. I see no chipmunks. I don't even see a turkey buzzard! Nearby, Purgatory's shallow stream runs as dark and sluggish as molasses in January. Without the moon, the world's become a sad and lifeless place.

She's been gone for over six days now.

I sit alongside Wild Bill and I stroke his bristly head. He's a noble hog—carrying me every which way. He's worn-out. I'm worn-out, too. We're two weary worn-out souls. We've traveled through WHITE SPACE twice with little food and no sleep.

I share stale corn bread with Wild Bill.

We share Milo's cup of cold tea.

Wild Bill stretches out on his side to nap. I curl up on the ground with my back against Wild Bill for warmth. He don't seem to mind. Head pillowed on my arm, I breathe in time to Wild Bill's breath—in and out, in and out.

I sleep—I don't know how long—maybe a minute, maybe an hour. The next thing I know something's licking my cheek.

I brush it away.

It licks my cheek again.

I swat at it.

"That's no way to greet an old friend," a deep voice grumbles.

I open my eyes to see Milo's dog Talker looking down at me with sad dark eyes. *Talker's here?* I sit bolt upright. Wild Bill sleeps on. Talker don't look right. He looks like a ghost dog. His light brown fur has turned as gray as ashes. I can see through the tips of his long ears.

He's fading away.

I say, "Talker, did you just talk to me?" He ain't never talked to me—only to Milo.

"I did," he grumbles. "I've been talking to you ever since I got back from chasing rabbits. In Purgatory, I chase rabbits, but I never catch one. That's the way it is here. You try and try again, but you never succeed. And now, I've come back expecting to find Milo here and I find you."

"Well, I'm sorry about that." I'm sorry about a

heap of things, including the fact that I've come all the way to Purgatory and my brother's not here!

"Where's Milo?" I hope he ain't as ghostly gray as Talker.

"Not with me," Talker grumbles. "He should be. A dog and his boy belong together. But he sent me out to chase rabbits and so I did. He went out searching for foot-wood. He says if he can find the right wood for making himself a foot—not too hard, not too soft—he can carve it, put it on and then travel to a DARK DARK PLACE I don't want him to go to, but he says he must."

"What DARK DARK PLACE?" I thought Milo wanted to climb the crystal staircase to High Jerusalem and play at God's Fall Jubilee. High Jerusalem's not dark. I'm told that place is bright with glory.

"It's all in THE AGE-OLD PROPHECY," Talker grumbles.

"What AGE-OLD PROPHECY?" It had better not be the one I heard earlier. I back up against Wild Bill for warmth and security. That tired old boar sleeps on.

"It's the one about how Magpie with the BLACK AND WHITE HAIR must lead BROWN TEETH and WHITE TEETH and THE ONE WITH NO TEETH AT ALL into a DARK DARK PLACE—THE PLACE OF THE BURIED MOON," Talker grumbles.

"That can't be THE PROPHECY!" I shriek.

"Well it is! We heard it from the wolves," Talker snaps.

"Well, I don't believe it." I refuse to believe it.

"Milo told me you'd say that," Talker grumbles. "Milo said, 'Talker, Magpie won't want to play her part in THE AGE-OLD PROPHECY. It goes against her grain. But I'm hoping and praying that, in the long run, she'll rise to the occasion. I want to be there to cheer her on with my music when she does.'"

"Milo said that?" The way Talker spoke, he sounded just like my brother.

"He did. He wants to play his hands for you in that DARK DARK PLACE. He wants to play them gloriously on key. That's why he's off now—searching for foot-wood. He's made eleven feet so far. None have worked. Seeing as how we're in Purgatory, I reckon none of them ever will." Talker looks mournfully at the foot pile.

"Milo don't need to be making himself no foot!" I take out the real one from my apron pocket. Talker sniffs the foot from toe to heel.

"That's Milo's," Talker grumbles. "But I don't see how he can reattach it. The foot's too solid and Milo's starting to fade like me."

Chapter Thirty-three

The Glue That Holds Us Together

ll this time I'd thought Milo could just put his foot back on. I hadn't figured on his slowly fading into a ghost while his foot remained so solid and full of life. For several long and miserable moments, I don't know what to do. And then a possible solution comes to me. I pour a dollop of Green Water into Milo's cup while explaining things to Talker. When I'm done, he shakes his mournful head and says, "This won't work."

"It has to work!" I shriek.

Wild Bill raises his head. He gives Talker and me the eye—*How dare you awaken me?* I talk in a lower tone, telling Talker exactly what the Red-Haired Girl told me—that Green Water is fired by love. There's nothing more powerful than love. Love is the glue that holds us together. Green Water will glue Milo's foot to his leg and make them all of a piece. It will! It has to.

"Tell Milo this." I poke Talker's chest to make sure I've got his full attention. *He feels softer than air.* "Tell him once he glues his foot back on, he's to hightail it to the spot where the Cob Hollow Path leads off from the Squabble Town Road." I do some calculating in my head—figuring in my days and days of travel. "Tell him Magpie—along with the rest of his family—will meet him there at dusk on October sixteenth and then, we'll all venture into that DARK DARK PLACE together."

This seems fitting.

This seems right.

All of us together.

"Did you say October sixteenth?" Talker grumbles.

"Yes, I did. I know that's everybody's deadline but I can't help the timing. I've got BROWN TEETH to talk to. I've got WHITE TEETH to talk to. To say nothing of the ONE WITH NO TEETH AT ALL. I don't know how I'll do all this by October sixteenth, but tell Milo, just knowing he'll be there at the end and playing his music for us means I'll try."

"I'll tell him," Talker grumbles.

Before I wind up Wild Bill yet again, I feed the tired old boar, still lying on his side, another handful of my grandpa's honey. Wild Bill laps it up. He grunts for more. I give him a second handful. Then, ever mindful of his heart, I slip in the key and wind him up real careful-like. When I'm done, he heaves himself onto his trotters and stands there, swaying.

I wish I could give him a third handful of honey, but I'll need it for the final leg of our journey—that being from them Sizemores and on home to Gabbard Mountain.

That's provided them Sizemores don't kill me first.

Why do I have to be the one to do all this?

It always seems to come down to me!

I mount Wild Bill while Talker looks on.

Wild Bill sinks to the ground.

I stare through Wild Bill's ears at Milo's pile of feet. Them feet are as sorry looking as this situation Wild Bill and I are in. He's worn-out from traveling. I don't want to be visiting Sizemores. They killed my grandpa's poor cows! Lord knows what they'll do to me.

I ain't never gonna save the moon.

A frown settles over me like a thunistated

A frown settles over me like a thundercloud.

"Milo says a happy face gets you places faster than a grumpy one," Talker grumbles.

"What do you know about happy faces?" I ask this mournful dog.

He bares his yellow teeth at me. This sorrowful old dog's trying to grin. It's so pitiful, I grin back. That grin sets something loose inside my brain. Why, it's a BRIGHT IDEA. It floats up into my forehead and, in spite of all my misery, settles there. It's the kind of BRIGHT IDEA Milo would come up with.

I grab hold of Wild Bill's ears, which brings him upright once again. I tell him, "Wild Bill, take me to a Sizemore boy. One who, like Milo, loves all animals no matter how mournful they might be. I want a boy who wouldn't dare to shoot a cow even though it was eating up his entire corn crop. This boy should live on Sizemore Propertee near Squabble Town, Kentucky, where there'll be ripe apples and juicy grubs for you to eat."

It takes Wild Bill some time to take this in.

I repeat my command.

Wild Bill rises with a flourish. He trots out along the little stream bank—gathering speed for the take-off. I call back to Talker, "Don't forget to give Milo his foot, the Green Water and my message." I can't hear Talker's answer because Wild Bill has broken into his bone-cracking run. I grip his sides. I tell myself, "Magpie Gabbard, you've got the fate of the world resting on your shoulders. Don't give up now."

Chapter Thirty-four

The Boy

Wild Bill dumps me off in a small wooded ravine—not far from a passel of Sizemore young 'uns, six girls and a boy. How do I know they're Sizemores? All have their mouths wide open in surprise at my sudden arrival on a wild boar's back. All have brown teeth.

"A Goblin! Run for your life!" the littlest girl shrieks.

"I ain't no Goblin. Do I look like one?" I scramble to my feet. I look myself over in fear that something might have changed in me as I was traveling through WHITE SPACE. I look the same as always—in my dark purple dress and white apron.

Them young 'uns scatter, all but the boy. Them scattering girls don't run like normal folk. They hop.

They hop three times on one foot. They hop three times on the other. They hop off into the surrounding brush—all the while spitting over their left shoulders.

It's almost the strangest sight I ever saw.

Wild Bill, no doubt satisfied he's brought me to the right place, roots up a rotted log. He noses underneath it—looking for grubs to eat.

I turn to the boy. He stands over something on the ground. I slowly approach the boy—tall, real skinny and he's got a shock of brown hair crowning his head.

He looks pale and tired.

I do myself some calculating—it's been ten days since them Goblins buried the moon. This no doubt means ten dark nights full of Goblins knock, knock, knocking at Sizemores' doors—*Let us in, we're hungry.* How can anyone sleep with that? I know us Gabbards can't.

The boy positions himself until he's between me and the something on the ground. Why, it's a little golden-haired dog. I see it now, lying dead-like between the boy's two bare feet.

"What happened to your dog?" When I ask, I'm careful not to show my teeth. I don't want anyone guessing at my Gabbard identity until the time is ripe.

"You know what happened." The boy glares at me like I'm the cause of it all.

"Well, I don't know, but I reckon I can guess." I stare around me at the trees—droopy looking in the pale still afternoon. There's a smell of Goblin in the air. "My guess is that a Goblin bit it."

"This dog ain't no it. She's my Sadie." The boy edges sideways so's I can get a peek at Sadie. She's got curly gold hair on top of her head, long ears and brown eyes—one looking up at me—blank-like and staring. She reminds me of the way Sweet Daddy looked right before I left him.

I hope Sweet Daddy's still alive.

I sink down to my heels. I pet Sadie's soft curly hair. Tears for Sweet Daddy and this whole sad situation pool in my eyes.

I hate them Goblins.

"The Goblin bit her sometime early this morning, near daylight." The boy has a clear, low and appealing voice. It reminds me of Milo's—the kind of easy voice you could listen to for hours. Who'd have thought a Sizemore would have a voice like this? He says, "My pappy wanted to put Sadie out of her misery, but I wouldn't let him. I carried her out here to the woods. I don't know what I figured on doing with her, but I couldn't let Pappy shoot her. Not when she's still got life. I won't let no Goblin have her neither. I'd die first." The boy lowers himself so he's alongside me, petting his dog.

She flaps her tail against the cold hard ground.

I told Wild Bill to take me to a boy who loves animals and he has.

"I got something that might help your Sadie." I unsling the flask the Red-Haired Girl filled for me six days ago. It's hard to believe six days have passed. "It's a miracle cure—Green Water."

"Doc Buckle's Green Water? I heard he was out of it. Has been for weeks," the boy says.

"That's why you saw me riding Wild Bill." I toss my head toward the old boar—eating grubs. "I rode him to Eastern Tennessee to get Green Water in order to save my Sweet Daddy's life.

"A Goblin attacked my Sweet Daddy, too," I say.

"You think Green Water will cure Sadie?" the boy says.

"If it don't, both your Sadie and my Sweet Daddy are in trouble." I uncap the flask. "Open her mouth so's I can slip a gurgle down her throat."

As the boy cradles his dog's head in his arms, I hear a rustle of leaves. I look up to see that passel of girls hopping and spitting toward the boy, his dog and me. They must have figured out I ain't no Goblin.

I don't smile at their approach. I can't show off my teeth just yet. These girls don't look happy about my being here. The one in the lead—the tallest, with a nose as sharp as a hawk's bill—looks downright mean.

"We're dosing Sadie with Green Water. So don't you shout at me nor carry on. You'll startle her," I say.

Them girls crowd in—hopping and spitting.

These Sizemore gals are a peculiar bunch.

The boy opens up Sadie's mouth, revealing her soft pink tongue and sharp white teeth. Coming in from the side, I pour Green Water down the dog's throat. The boy shuts her mouth so she can't spit up the cure. I cap the flask.

The dog closes her eyes.

The dog slumps in her boy's arms.

"You've killed Sadie!" the tallest girl shrieks.

"But Green Water's supposed to be a cure! It ain't supposed to hurt anyone. I was going to use it on my own Sweet Daddy. My brother, too," I wail.

"You meant to kill Sadie!" The tallest girl launches herself at me. I find myself knocked to the ground. She throws herself on top of me. Well, that ain't nice and here I was, just trying to be kind. I knee her in the stomach. I kick her off me only to have them other five girls pile on. They yell at me, "You killed Sadie!"

"I meant to help her!" I shriek into their yards of dirty calico. It don't do no good. I pummel them with my fists. They pull at my hair. The tall one, back in the fray, rubs dirt into my cheek. There's shrieking and carrying on and now barking fit to die.

Barking?

The tallest girl—Old Hawk Nose—backs off and suddenly I've got the fury of a golden-haired dog at my face—her bared teeth just inches from my nose. *Sadie!* I reckon the Green Water knocked her out in order to bring her back in fighting Sizemore form. I tell you—never has the sight of an attacking dog looked so sweet. Nor has a boy—this shock-topped, dark-eyed boy—now pulling that dog off me.

Chapter Thirty-five

Doing the Unthinkable

Well, the tallest girl, the one with the nose, is named Darlene Sizemore, only she goes by the name of Hawk. It figures. Her five younger sisters all have names that begin with the letter *D*—Doanna, Dora, Daisy, Delilah and Dewdrop—she's the littlest.

The boy's name is Duby. I like Duby. I'd always been told there was nothing good about Sizemores. I was told wrong. There's something deep-down good about this boy. I hope I get to know him better. He grins up at me from where he now sits with a smiling Sadie in his lap. I'd grin back but I can't reveal my identity until after I've told them all about THE AGE-OLD PROPHECY. I haven't had a moment to launch into that because Hawk's taken it upon herself to teach me the "Hop and Spit." Hawk says it will protect me from Goblins who've been plaguing Squabble Town for the past ten nights.

It's been ten nights.

Hawk learned the "Hop and Spit" technique three days ago from a "Hop and Spit" preacher who'd been passing through Squabble Town.

This is the "Hop and Spit."

You start with your right foot. You hop on it once—that's for sunlight. You hop on it twice—that's for firelight. You hop on it a third time—that's for starlight. Then, with all this light called on to keep you safe from Goblins, you spit over your left shoulder—that means, *So be it, amen!* You repeat all the above on the left foot, then again on the right and so on.

Hawk says the upside to the "Hop and Spit" is that it's not that hard to do—provided you can do it without tripping. The downside is that hopping everywhere can grow tiresome, besides which, with all that spitting, you can spit yourself dry and where will you be then?

"Are you sure it works?" I say.

"The preacher says so. But I ain't about to go outside after dark and hop and spit my way past Goblins to test it for myself," Hawk says.

"Where's the moon whose light used to keep us safe?" little Dewdrop wails.

"Well, I'll tell you," I say. "Them Goblins buried her—not all that far from here—in Cob Hollow. They've buried her alive. I saw her struggling. She cried out, 'Help me.' I saw it all—in my granny's prophesying kettle."

At Hawk's look of disbelief, I go on, "It was that selfsame kettle that sent me to the girl who gave me the Green Water, which saved your Sadie's life."

We look at Sadie—wiggling on her back while Duby rubs her stomach. This Duby don't say much, but I can tell he's taking things in by the deep and thoughtful look that's come over his dark eyes.

"That Green Pond Girl has the second sight," I tell everyone. "She's seen the buried moon for herself. She told me there's but one way we can save her."

"What's that way?" Hawk says.

I tell them all about THE AGE-OLD PROPHECY and when I'm done, all their mouths—except for Duby's—are wide open in astonished horror.

"There ain't no way I'm holding hands with a white-toothed Gabbard!" Hawk shrieks. "If I were to touch a Gabbard, I'd keel over then and there and die."

"We'd all die!" them other five shout.

"I understand your thinking," I tell them

153

Sizemore girls. Oh, I do understand. It wears me out to think about it. If it were just me, I'd walk away from this right now. But I have the fate of the world resting on my shoulders. So I rise above the legacy of fussing and fighting that my grandpa passed on to me and I do the unthinkable—I grab up Hawk's hands the same way the Red-Haired Girl once grabbed up mine. I say, "Hawk, do you know who I am?"

"You're THE GIRL WITH THE BLACK AND WHITE HAIR who says she's supposed to lead BROWN TEETH and WHITE TEETH on a suicide mission," Hawk says.

"I'm also Margaret Magpie Gabbard—come to tell you that if you don't join my family in freeing the moon, we all might as well go hopping and spitting to an early grave." To prove my identity, I show Hawk my snow-white teeth.

Hawk faints. It takes some time to revive her. Hawks pats herself to make sure she's still alive while Duby takes the reins. Duby, the good and kind Sizemore, says to me, "Don't you worry. I'll gather thirteen Sizemores to help you out. I'll bring the best."

"No guns," I say.

"No guns," he assures me.

Chapter Thirty-six

Another Hurdle
to Overcome

fter winding up Wild Bill yet again, I mount him for what I hope will be the final time. It had better be! If I could, I'd walk him up the mountain, but it is too late in the day for that. And I can't be spending the night with Sizemores. It's hard enough just talking to them, except for Duby. I like him.

You'd think I'd feel triumphant—I've got Duby Sizemore committed to my cause. But I've also got a tired Wild Bill sagging beneath me and yet another hurdle to overcome—my family. Will they hold hands with Sizemores and unite with them to free the moon? What about Sweet Daddy and Randall? Are they still alive?

I stroke Wild Bill's trembling neck. I tell him,

"Wild Bill, don't give up on me now." Then I scream into his ears something I know he'll like—"Take me to my Grandpa Gabbard's bee gum! I promise you honey and sweet apples to eat. And then, you can curl up in your own nest in the bramble patch and sleep."

Wild Bill don't need nothing better than that. He trots off with me. Duby waves good-bye. I wave back. Wild Bill breaks into his bone-cracking run. We lift off into WHITE SPACE. Before I know it, I'm landing, bottoms down, on Gabbard Mountain—right beside the bee gum where, it seems, my journey first began.

There's a funny thing about that bee gum. It's not quiet the way it was when I approached it on my thirteenth birthday. The bee gum's alive with angry swarming bees. Is this because the moon's been buried for thirteen days and their entire world's been thrown off-kilter on account of it?

It's been thirteen days.

There's no way I'm getting honey for Wild Bill from that angry-looking bee gum. I'd be stung to death. On all fours, I back away with the boar snuffling after me. I crawl backward to an old apple tree. Safe behind it, I break open Granny's honey gourd against the tree trunk. I give Wild Bill the honey that's left. While the boar tears into that, I shinny up the tree and pick all the apples I can reach. I throw these down for Wild Bill so that he can have himself a well-earned feast.

I tell Wild Bill, "When dark comes, you hunker down in that nest you got in the bramble patch. I don't want Goblins carrying you off." As if Goblins could. Wild Bill would be more than a match for them! "I'll be back." I give the boar a friendly slap on the neck and then, I race off for my cabin.

It's drawing onto dusk. Leaves, still hanging from our trees, are the bruised color of Goblin skin. I hear the sound of a distant THWOCK, which means them Goblins are rising in their faraway hollow. I catch the drift of wood smoke. I reckon Big Mama's had to burn herself a heap of wood fires night after night to keep them Goblins away from our cabin.

If she kept them away.

I race over the crest of the hill. I see, down below, a dark plume of smoke rising from our cabin chimney—a sure sign of life. I can't wait to see my family. As I race down the hill, the smoke quickly forms six words:

MAGPIE! YOU'D BETTER GET
HOME NOW!

Chapter Thirty-seven
Us Gabbards

ranny Goforth's the only one on our mountain who has a prophesying kettle that can form smoke words and send them up a chimney. Granny must have moved herself and her kettle into our cabin to help out my Big Mama while I've been gone. If they've been using that kettle to spy on me and my adventures, I reckon they got an eyeful.

I can't be worried about that!

As I scramble down the stony bank behind our outhouse, I hear Goblins thwocking themselves out of their faraway lairs—THWOCK, THWOCK, THWOCK. I also hear THWOCKS coming from spots that don't sound quite so faraway. Are Goblins establishing lairs on Gabbard Mountain? This can't be good.

I duck through sheltering hemlocks and into our yard. I don't see any chickens scratching in the dirt for mealy bugs. My family's probably brought them inside. After all, it's nearly dark. I see long narrow footprints dragged through the dust—*Goblin footprints.* I see scratch marks on our front door—*Goblin marks.* I smell Goblin rotgut—enough to curl my nose hairs.

If them Goblins have hurt my family, I swear, I'll kill them Goblins single-handedly, one by one. I fling wide my cabin door. I'm greeted by a flurry of squawking chickens, burning pine knots and my family—Gabbards and Goforths—shrieking, "You're here! You're finally here!"

I shriek, "I brought the Green Water!"

"We knew you was bringing it," Thelma shrieks in my ear. "We've been following you in Granny's kettle. She set it up in the kitchen. We'd yell at the kettle, 'Show us Magpie, where is she?' and it would. We watched you every which place you went and when you was flying through WHITE SPACE, we'd go back to visit the places you'd been.

"It's sad about the Head," Thelma says.

"What happened to the Head?" I shriek.

"Them Goblins got mad at it. They swung it through briars. They kicked it through dirt. Then they hurled it back into the well. The last time we saw the Head, it was deep underwater. It looked like it was settling in for a good long mope."

"They must have found out he gave me the key for getting fast to the Red-Haired Girl," I say.

"That's what we figured," Lazarus, on my other side, says. "We saw it all. I felt real sorry for the Head, even though he killed our great-great-grandfather."

"I ain't so sure he did. I'll get even with them Goblins!" I shriek.

"You're not getting even with anyone. At least not yet." Big Mama swoops me up in her warm arms. In all the crush, I hadn't seen Big Mama. She says into my right ear, "Magpie Gabbard, I got a bone to pick with you. But for right now, I'm just glad you're back." She near about squeezes me to death. I hang there, soaking up her warmth. I'll need it for the bone picking ahead.

When she finally releases me, Big Mama pulls me past Uncle Henry, Granny Goforth and then, Randall. He looks as gritless as ever. He whispers in my ear, "Did you get to see Milo?"

"I didn't," I whisper back. "But don't worry. We'll see him soon."

"We will?" Randall looks like a boy who's been

promised a fortune in gold and silver. I can't deny him that. And so, even though I'm not altogether sure we'll see Milo, I say, "We will."

Big Mama pulls me over to Sweet Daddy. I hadn't seen him, sitting quietly in his rocking chair over by the fireplace. He has a dog keeping watch on either side of him. He don't even look up at my approach.

Goblins did this to him.

"All he's done since you left is stare at his hands," Big Mama says.

"At least he's still alive." I uncork the flask of Green Water that I pray will heal him.

Aunt Louisa shoves two cups into my face to pour that Green Water into. She hisses at me, "You took your time returning home to your ailing kin."

"Magpie had her reasons," Granny Goforth says.

I send Granny Goforth a grateful smile.

Granny smiles back.

Before pouring the Green Water, I say to everyone who's gathered round, "While you watched me in Granny's kettle, you no doubt saw me give Green Water to a dog, after which that dog keeled over like it was dead.

"I want you to remember—that dog rose again."

"That was a Sizemore dog," Aunt Louisa snaps.

"Yes it was," I snap right back. I feel ready to take her on. I'm ready to take on anyone or anything. I've been to the Floating Head, the Green Pond, Purgatory, them Sizemores and now, back here and I'm still not done. I fill the first cup with Green Water. I give it to Randall. I want to see how he handles the cure before giving it to Sweet Daddy—so pale and weak.

Randall says, "Thank you, Magpie."

"Drink up, Randall." I hope the Green Water will even him out. I don't want a gritless Randall. I don't want him the way he became after Milo left us—downright mean. I just want Randall the way he used to be—strong and helpful.

Randall drinks his cup dry. He don't keel over like Sadie did. However, as Randall stands there, a look of sudden understanding appears to come over him—like the entire world, including me, has been made clear.

I don't have time to ponder what this might mean.

I fill the second cup for Sweet Daddy. I hand it to him. Big Mama, at Sweet Daddy's back, holds on to his shoulders to steady him. She knows this could be hard on him. Sweet Daddy drinks the Green Water. I wait for him to keel over. He don't neither. But that's us Gabbards. You think we're gonna do one thing. We do another.

Chapter Thirty-eight

A Force to Contend With

Several moments after draining his cup dry, Sweet Daddy looks at me and he says my name—"Magpie." It's the sweetest sound I ever heard. I drop to my knees in front of him. He grabs hold of my two hands. He squeezes them and says, "I have something to tell you."

"Not now! You need to rest!" Big Mama shrieks.

"Rosie, I need to talk." Sweet Daddy's voice don't sound weak the way you'd think it might after not being used for days. His voice sounds as strong as ever. *Green Water's a miracle cure.* He says, "Something terrible has happened to the moon."

"We know, Sweet Daddy. We saw her in Granny's prophesying kettle." I want to make this easy for him.

"It's on account of me." Tears well in Sweet

Daddy's eyes. I gently squeeze his trembling hands. Oh, I hate to see him sad. He says, "I was on my way home from Doc's. It was growing dark. I ran across the bridge into Cob Hollow. I ran through the Hall of the Goblin King. Just as I was through that hall, I paused to catch my breath—near some boulders. It's then I heard a Goblin say:

> *Fee, fi, fo, fan,*
> *I smell the blood of an earthly man.*

"I lit out like greased lightning, but that wasn't fast enough. A Goblin leapt onto my back. It sunk its eyeteeth into my neck." Sweet Daddy releases my hands. Rubbing the spot where that Goblin bit him, he says, "I tried to fight it off. I grew weaker and weaker.

"And then, all of a sudden, there was the moon. She'd come down to Cob Hollow to stand at my side at her time of weakness when she's supposed to rest." He looks up at us as if to make sure we're taking this in. *We are.* "She shook her head, throwing off her hood. I've never seen such a glorifying, such a terrifying brightness. The Goblin retreated from it—back into its dark and evil world.

"The moon told me, 'Sweets, you'd better get on home. I'll light your way.' I never thought she was in danger. I was in a weakened state myself and mazed by her light. All I could think of was home. So I ran. I followed the path my beloved moon lit up for me. And then, her light dimmed. I turned. I saw Goblins. Goblins had snuck up behind the moon—on her dark side. They'd pushed her down. Now they climbed all over her, shoving her down, down, down. She cried out to me, 'Run, Sweets, run!'

"I ran. But what else could I do? And the night turned black as pitch. The black night filled with Goblin voices. Thousands of voices crowed how Goblins had buried the moon. How the night, after hundreds of years of trying, would now be theirs forever.

"I ran and ran. In my weakened state, I must have run myself senseless, for I knew nothing more until now—awakening to see my Magpie here before me." Tears stream down Sweet Daddy's cheeks. "If the moon hadn't come to earth and saved my life, she'd be in our sky now—glowing soft and golden.

"She saved my life," Sweet Daddy sobs.

"And we'll save her." I look up from him to all my relations. "I know the way. It's come down to me through an AGE-OLD PROPHECY. If everyone will listen up and give me time to talk without interruption, I'll explain it." Even as I'm saying this, there comes an interruption.

Goblins—knock, knock, knocking on our door:

> *Magpie, Magpie, let us in.*
> *We'll show you the hairs on our chinny*
>   *chin chin.*
> *We'll give you a crown, a robe made of bone*
> *We'll make you our queen*
> *Our Darkness—your throne.*

They ain't never called me by name and now they're offering to make me their queen? Now that's something. They must have figured out what I've been up to and that I'm a force to contend with.

Well, I am.

Chapter Thirty-nine
The Truth Comes Out

We've got this cabin so well lit, you'd think
we had the moon herself glowing here
inside. The cow's skull glows. Pine knots
flare in the two windows. The fireplace blazes and
candles are lit everywhere. We'll keep them all burning until the sun finally reappears, once more driving
them infernal Goblins into hiding.

Our fourteen hogs, three mules, two horses,
two entire flocks of sheep and five milk cows are
safe in the Hidey-Hole for the night. Thirty-seven
chickens settle in the loft above. The day I left our
mountain, Granny Goforth brought her kettle and
her family to this cabin to help out Big Mama.
Granny brought the livestock as well. They've stayed
here ever since—taking shelter in the Hidey-Hole at

night and going out in daylight to take in fresh air and food.

But someone always has to be outside with the livestock even during the day. Someone has to keep them away from the dark places—like the deep woods and shadowed dips between the hilly pastures.

Goblins hide out in them places now.

It used to be they'd retreat to Cob Hollow when the sun rose. They'd stay in that hollow until the next moonless night. We could depend on that. Now, with the buried moon, they own every night. They hide out in any dark place they can find until that night descends.

It's nighttime now.

We're settled in the front room. We're waiting for Thelma to return from using the chamber pot. Then, even though Goblins prowl outside this cabin, I'm to tell everyone in whispers how we are to save the moon.

On our front porch, Goblins fuss through Big Mama's cloth poke in which she stores stray chicken feathers. As they do, they jabber:

> *One-ery, two-ery,*
> *Ziccary Zan.*
> *Hollow bone, crack a bone,*

Fast as you can.
Twiddledum, twaddledum,
Nine-ery ten.
Suck out the marrow.
Let's start again!

Them fool Goblins know chicken feathers don't have no marrow! They're counting feathers with that silly rhyme to scare us. I hear other Goblins settle themselves on our wood box. Others fret at the front window—*Magpie, Magpie, let us in. . . .* With the moon buried, them Goblins have grown bolder than ever.

Randall stands at the outskirts of our group—the rest of us sitting in a half circle facing the blazing fire while waiting for Thelma to reappear. Randall ain't spoken but a few words since he drank Green Water. He said them to Big Mama—"You don't need to fuss over me. I'm fine."

Now, leaning against Big Mama's china hutch, Randall rubs his hairless nose while studying me. I ain't never had Randall study me. But, then again, Goblins ain't never asked me to be their queen. I reckon that must make me someone special in my brother's eyes.

"I'm back." Thelma slips into her spot beside me.

"Before Magpie begins, I need to talk," Big Mama says. She's seated beside Sweet Daddy. They're holding hands—two loving parents united against their daughter. I reckon I'm in for that bone picking now.

"This is important. It concerns Milo's foot," Big Mama says.

With Big Mama, it always comes down to that foot. Won't she ever let it go? She says that up to the moment she saw—in Granny's kettle—me taking Milo's foot out of my apron pocket at his sycamore, Big Mama hadn't realized the foot was gone. "I couldn't believe it was gone!" she says. "I ran from Granny's kettle and into the front room, hoping to see that foot on its Hallowed Spot.

"I found goldenrods there." Big Mama looks square on at me. "I went back to the kettle. There was the foot. The last time I looked in the kettle, Talker was using Milo's foot to rest his muzzle on."

"I hope by now, that foot's on Milo," I say.

"If it is, he's hoofing it to High Jerusalem. We'll never see him again. And here you didn't want him leaving us any more than I did," Big Mama wails.

"None of us wanted Milo to leave," Randall says real quiet-like. I look over at him. Randall ain't lounging against the china hutch now. He's standing up straight—on his own. He says, "I tried to make him stay here, too. Didn't I help to lock him up? I see now that wasn't right. It was his time to go and I didn't let him. That was selfish of me and I'm sorry about that. I only wish I could see him again to tell him so."

"You'll get to see him," I tell Randall.

"I will?" He gives me a wondering look that says I'm to tell it to him straight, No pussyfooting around. Looks like the Green Water did its job—looks like Randall's got his grit back. I like this Randall. It's the old Randall. The one who built a water system with me.

"We all will." I go on to explain what's been going on with Milo and how, once he gets his foot back on, he wants to join us in that DARK DARK PLACE, the place of the buried moon. As I'm talking, I keep my eyes pinned on Randall and he keeps his eyes pinned on me. And I feel as if it's just the two of us—Randall and Magpie—alone in the cabin and speaking head-to-head about our favorite brother who wants to help us out in the one way he knows how . . . playing his hands.

And the feeling is good.

The way it was before Milo left us.

"Magpie," Sweet Daddy says once I'm done talking about Milo—as if I ever could be done—"how are we to save the moon?"

I lean into the circle of my family. I drop my voice to a whisper. "Tomorrow, at dusk, we must all be at the entrance to the Cob Hollow Path—Milo will meet us there." *I hope.*

"Now this next part will be a little hard to stomach. But I can't help that. It's part of THE AGE-OLD PROPHECY that's been passed down through these mountains for years.

"We need twenty-six people to bravely venture forth into Cob Hollow just before night descends. It's in Cob Hollow that we'll find the buried moon—trapped beneath a giant stone. We need twenty-six people to break the Goblins' spell—binding stone to earth. Twenty-six people need to hold hands in a circle around the stone. They need to hold hands and shout blessings. Thirteen of these people must be us Gabbards." I pause. I let the rest out all at once—"TheotherthirteenmustbeSizemores."

"Sizemores?" Big Mama says.

"That's right, Big Mama," I say.

"I'm not holding hands with Sizemores! Duck Sizemore poisoned Randall!" Big Mama says.

"Duck didn't poison Randall," I say as Thelma elbows me—*Magpie, don't tell.* I take a deep breath, for now comes the hardest part of all—it no doubt will ruin whatever good's come between Randall and me, but it needs to be said. "Duck didn't poison Randall, because I did."

"If Magpie did that, then I did it, too," Thelma says.

Randall stands there, looking stunned.

His sister and his sweetheart poisoned him.

Chapter Forty

With Stones in Our Mouths

It's midafternoon—October 16th. We've locked the livestock in the Hidey-Hole to keep them safe during the dangerous night ahead. Granny's covered over her kettle so that it can take a well-deserved rest and now all thirteen of us Gabbard Mountain folk—young, old, male and female—hurry down our mountain slope.

Early this morning, Big Mama had asked to see, in Granny's kettle, where Milo and his foot had got to. Were they together now? If so, was Milo headed toward the Cob Hollow Path? Or was he climbing the crystal staircase up to High Jerusalem? I wanted to know myself!

Granny fired up her kettle. We all looked on. I could hardly wait to see Milo—walking square on his two feet—as complete as he'd been before I went and told Big Mama on him. I wanted to see Milo's easy stride and his smile to match it. I planned to reach into the kettle's bubbling water. Even though I'd get burned, I'd planned to tap Milo on his shoulder and see that smile when he looked up and saw it was me.

Would he have a smile for me?

But no matter how often and loud Granny yelled at her kettle, "Show us Milo. *Where is he?*" all she got was milk white steam. No one dared venture what this might mean although I did wonder aloud, did folks see this same steam those times they tried to call me up in Granny's kettle while I was traveling through WHITE SPACE.

Thelma answered, "We could always see you, Magpie. You and Wild Bill—galloping across what looked like an endless white sheet."

"Perhaps Milo's moved on to High Jerusalem," Sweet Daddy said.

"No, he hasn't!" I shrieked. "He told Talker he'd meet us in the Hollow and he will!"

Now we're headed down the mountain with Big Mama in the lead—Sweet Daddy a few steps behind her. Big Mama strides through the stale cold air, a rope wrapped around her waist. After Milo joins us—

if he joins us—and after we save the moon—*if we save the moon*—Big Mama plans to hog-tie Milo and haul him on home.

I told her, "Big Mama, you can't haul Milo home."

She said, "Oh yes I can."

The afternoon shadows gather as we scramble down our mountain. Tree limbs arch across the path—their leaves hanging dark and heavy. Earlier, Sweet Daddy told me, "If those trees don't let go of their dead leaves, there'll be no room for new buds in the spring."

Cheerful Creek's dried up. Now it's nothing but sun-baked dirt with rocks and boulders, jumbled up, one against the other. Thelma's warned me, "Don't go near them boulder piles. Goblins could be hiding out in them."

Just two days ago, Thelma had gone to the springhouse with a pail of milk. It was the middle of the day. No sooner did she step into that cool dark springhouse than a clammy HAND grabbed her foot. A GOBLIN'S HAND. Thelma knew instantly by the smell.

Thelma threw milk at THAT HAND.

THAT HAND let her go.

Thelma told me, "I ain't never going near that springhouse ever again!"

And who can blame her?

Thelma now has her arm linked in mine. We follow Big Mama and Sweet Daddy down the mountain as the sun sinks lower in the sky. Aunt Louisa and Uncle Henry, with Granny Goforth between them, follow along behind us. Them five Goforth brothers and Randall bring up the rear.

Randall ain't spoken one word to me since last night.

And here, after Big Mama castigated Thelma and me for poisoning him, we both told Randall how sorry we were.

Thelma told Randall, "I was only trying to sweeten you up."

I told Randall, "You was acting mean to Thelma."

Randall told Thelma, "I reckon I was trying to tell you I wasn't the right man for you to marry and acting mean was the one way I knew how.

"I'm sorry about that, Thelma."

Thelma broke down and bawled. Randall patted her back and acted sweet to her. He said nothing to me.

What I did to him was wrong.

Throw me to the Goblins!

We're near about three quarters of our way down-mountain. Soon the path will dump us willy-nilly onto the Squabble Town Road. None of us are talking much. We got stones in our mouths. You ever try talking with a stone in your mouth?

Talking's not easy.

The stones are Sweet Daddy's idea.

Sweet Daddy said, "A stone in your mouth will remind you of the stone that weighs down our precious moon. It'll remind you to keep quiet. We don't want Goblins knowing that we plan to free her. They think they got us whipped. That us Gabbards are too busy quarreling among ourselves and poisoning each other to think about the moon.

"We'll fool them good."

We creep quietly and stealthily downhill.

"Loooth at thhhhat." Thelma tugs on my arm. She points to the left of the path where the earth has fallen away and you can see its innards—rock slabs jamming up against each other with tree roots hanging over them—forming a dirt-dark cave.

Something dark's curled up in that cave.

A Goblin.

We point it out to those behind us—*beware.*

We hurry onward. We head on down the mountain. As we do, I hear, over to my left, the sound of something—a Goblin?—following us. It skitters through the lengthening shadows to the left of our path—in the dark there—among the trees.

Chapter Forty-one

They Know What We're Up To

B y the time we turn onto the Squabble Town Road, we've got more than one Goblin tailing us. So far, Thelma and I have counted eleven. We haven't seen these Goblins—except for the first. But we've heard them—scurrying through last year's fallen leaves, in the shadowy woods, bordering the road.

Thelma and I have spit out our stones. With all these Goblins tailing us, we don't need stones to remind us to keep our mouths shut. The Goblins know we're up to something anyway. Why else would they be silently tailing us and here it's not even night-time yet?

Our group moves as one down the winding potholed road. As evening's shadows fall, we crowd together. Big Mama's curls bob up against my nose. I sneeze. I startle something. It scurries through the shadows beneath Sizemore apple trees.

"That makes twelve Goblins," Thelma whispers.

We make our way down the road, growing ever dimmer in the fading light. I don't see a turkey buzzard flapping among them apple trees like I did the last time I was here. Nor do I see that sign stuck to a tree trunk: *Sizemore Propertee—You Gabbards Keep Out!*

I wonder if Duby took it down?

I like Duby and I trust him. I know that one way or another he'll gather his kin together to help us save the moon—even if he has to hog-tie them and drag them here. I just know it.

By the time we reach the bend in the Squabble Town Road, where it curves sharply right and meanders another three miles before reaching town, Thelma and I have quietly counted thirteen Goblins tailing us—a Goblin to take on each of us. Ain't that nice? I wonder which Goblin means to take me on?

I now see, ahead of our group, a passel of Sizemores gathered at the entrance to the Cob Hollow Path. I count thirteen Sizemores—six grown-ups I've never met, Duby and his six sisters who are all hopping and spitting.

But them grown-up Sizemores don't look happy. Their eyes narrow as we approach. Not a one says "Howdy." I don't see any guns. *At least they don't have guns.* But if looks could kill, all us Gabbards would be dead.

I walk over to Duby, who looks as worried as I feel. I brace myself for hearing Tam Pierce's thin, high voice wailing out for pity and for his hog. Tam must know that we're nearby. His well's just on the other side of the laurel patch from where we are and Tam's got good ears.

As hard as I listen, I don't hear Tam.

Is he still down-under in that well water—moping his life away?

Or is he hiding out because he's afraid?

Chapter Forty-two

Moving On

Home has always been the hub of my world with spokes coming forth from it and going out across my wide and rolling mountaintop. I know that world. And those places I didn't know at first—those secret out-of-the-way places—Milo always showed me. He'd come across me on a day when he was feeling well enough to walk outside and he'd say to me, "Want to go someplace different?" I'd say, "Why, sure."

Once he took me to a cave on the south side of our mountain where bats would sleep away the daylight—upside down. Once he took me no farther away than beneath our Grandpa Gabbard's bed. There, not far from where Grandpa kept his multivolume set of *The Decline and Fall of the Roman Empire*, Milo showed me a door in the floor. Milo opened that door. He slipped down into the darkness and I followed after him. We dropped into a small earthen-floored room—off the Hidey-Hole—in which Grandpa hid his moonshine whiskey along with a cache of store-bought candy.

Milo and I shared a piece of Grandpa's candy. It was the best candy I ever ate—there, in the darkness, with Milo.

And when Grandma Gabbard died three years back and we had to bury her, Milo was the one who climbed into the open grave to help lower the pinewood coffin into it.

Milo said to me, "Come see what it's like down here."

So I scrambled in.

Milo showed me that there was nothing scary about the darkness of a grave. It's just a resting place for bones. As for Grandma Gabbard's spirit? Milo said it was up in High Jerusalem where Grandma was having herself a time—kicking up her heels and chewing tobacco.

Grandma Gabbard loved to chew tobacco.

And so I'd assumed that Milo would be with me as I gathered together two groups of people who've been fighting each other for years. I'd assumed he'd walk at my side as I led these anxious folks who mostly hate each other's guts down, down, down into a place I'd never been—the darkest place of all—Cob Hollow.

I assumed wrong.

Milo's not here.

Instead of Milo, I got Randall. Oh, he's got his grit back now. He's the old Randall—fearless in the face of sorrow.

After we'd greeted them Sizemores in the one way we knew how—sharing names—Randall said to all and sundry, including Big Mama, who was looking around for Milo while fiddling with her rope, "I reckon we'd better be heading out."

"Not without Milo," I said. I explained to them Sizemores just who Milo was—my other brother, who was coming here from Purgatory. He'd fire us on to do our best by playing his remarkable music. I noticed how Duby smiled when I said music. *He likes music.*

"We don't have time to wait for him, Magpie." Those were Randall's first words to me since I'd admitted to poisoning him. And here he'd wanted to be with Milo as much as I did! Randall said, "It's already dusk. We have to find the moon. Think of the moon."

Oh, I thought of the moon all right. Saw her in my mind's eye—struggling to be free. I knew we only had 'til midnight to help her. But I'd left the message for Milo to meet us here! As long as we waited at the entrance to the Cob Hollow Path, there was hope of seeing him.

And then Randall—his eyes on mine—stuck a knife blade in my heart. He said, "Maybe Milo couldn't put his foot back on. Or maybe he got lost. Or maybe he just wants us to do this on our own. Whatever it is, we need to move on, Magpie. We need to save the moon without him."

Chapter Forty-three

The Goblin King

It's growing so dark now I can barely make out the dirt path in front of me. That path can turn on a dime, so I have to keep my eyes on it—only looking right now and again in hopes of seeing a Goblin's blue lantern hanging from a dead tree.

The Green Pond Girl said, "Magpie, you got to look right."

Well, I'm trying.

The dimly lit path's so narrow we have to walk single file down it. I'm in the lead because I'm supposed to be. That's how THE AGE-OLD PROPHECY goes.

I've got WHITE TEETH following me.

I've got BROWN TEETH.

I've got Granny Goforth—THE ONE WITH NO TEETH AT ALL.

And I got Randall at my back.

Earlier, Randall whispered to me, "Magpie, if you need my help, you holler." I whispered back, "There ain't no way I'm calling on you. I wanted to wait for Milo and you wouldn't let me. I can't stand you, Randall."

He makes me so mad, I could spit.

The hollow's steep and rocky slopes squeeze me in on either side. It feels to me like the hollow itself wants to gobble me up. I'm nothing but a pea, caught up in Cob Hollow's giant jaws with teeth as large as boulders and no doubt sharper than Big Mama's butchering knife.

I lead everyone down a path that twists and turns like a writhing snake. I wave my hands before my face, breaking through cobwebs while all the time looking right. I don't see nothing. I walk on and on through the dark and smelly hollow. All I hear is twenty-six pairs of feet, kicking up gravel. Where are them Goblins? You'd think by now they'd be creeping up behind us:

> *And we'll beat you, beat you, beat you,*
> *And we'll beat you all to pap,*
> *And we'll eat you, eat you, eat you,*
> *Every morsel snap, snap, snap.*

I reckon they're waiting for the opportune time and then, they'll attack.

Bring them on.

The path beneath my feet turns muddy.

We ain't had no rain in fourteen days and here, we got mud.

Is this where them Goblins have had their lairs ever since they followed Great-Grandmother Margaret here from England?

Is this where they'd go THWOCK?

Raising skull-like heads—THWOCK?

Raising a bony arm—THWOCK?

Thousands of them going:

THWOCK, THWOCK, THWOCK, THWOCK, THWOCK?

I feel something breathing down my neck. It's Randall. I'm sure it's Randall, trying to act like a bossy big brother by keeping close to me. I DON'T NEED HIM! I turn to elbow him in the stomach—*Leave me alone*—and I hear something whisper in my right ear: *I'll give you a throne, a robe made of bone. . . .*

This don't sound like Randall. But in case it is, I turn to elbow him hard and I'm jerked off my feet and onto my stomach! I'm dragged, stomach down, off the path and into what feels like sticky muck.

This ain't funny!

"Randall, let me go!" I scream.

"I ain't got hold of you!" Randall says.

"You don't?" I turn to fight off whatever does and I almost wish I hadn't. I find myself in the grip of the Goblin King. I can just make out his crown of human finger bones. I catch the red glare of his evil eyes. He digs his fingernails into my shoulders—*Magpie, Magpie, let me in.* He opens his stinking mouth, his fangs bared, ready to sink themselves into my tender neck.

Gathering all the breath that I got in me, I holler out, "Randall, help me!" while jamming my right fist into the Goblin King's jaw—snap!

I lunge for the path and Randall grabs me under my arms. He lifts me out of the muck with the Goblin King hanging on to my knees. Randall lifts me higher and higher. Hands beneath my armpits, my strong, my gritty brother lifts me way up high like he did that time he helped me pick ripe apples.

"Why, thank you, Randall," I find myself saying and the Goblin King releases my knees, caterwauling as he falls.

And it's then I see, over Randall's left shoulder, a bright and glowing light.

And it ain't just no blue lantern light.

It's . . . Milo.

Chapter Forty-four

Milo

Randall carries me toward our brother. At his feet lies the giant stone holding down the moon. *She's here.* The dark feels alive with silent, watching Goblins. Why don't they attack? Are they afraid of Milo? He stands beneath the dead tree. The Goblin's blue lantern shines so dimly alongside him. Milo glows pure white—whiter than I've ever seen him even at his sickest when he lay in bed so pale and wrung out from his coughing.

He's so white now, he looks like he ain't a part of this world but the next. He stands square on his own two feet. *He's got his foot back on.* Talker peeks out from behind my brother. Milo's dog is as ghostly white as he is.

Milo gives us all his crooked grin.

Big Mama rushes up to hug him.

He puts up a warning hand—*Don't touch.*

Big Mama hugs herself—her eyes on him.

I feel a hard ache in my throat.

Randall puts me down. I gesture for Gabbards and Sizemores to come together to form a circle around the stone.

Folks don't move.

Folks just stand there staring at me. Here they followed me down down down into this Hollow. But they still ain't about to touch each other. Not even to save the moon.

I can see it's up to me. I drag Thelma to stand alongside Big John—Duby's uncle. I saw how Thelma blushed when them two met. I drag Randall next to Hawk—they could be a pair. I make sure each Goforth boy stands alongside a Sizemore girl. There's just enough of each. I drag Big Mama next to Sissy Sizemore—Duby's mama. Before you know it, I've got WHITE TEETH next to BROWN TEETH clear around the circle and down to Granny Goforth—THE ONE WITH NO TEETH AT ALL.

I place myself between Duby and his daddy, Duck.

Who'd have thought Duby's daddy would be Duck?

I look over at Milo. Tears fill my eyes. *He's here.*
I nod my head and Milo grins. He sets into playing
music soft and sweet and full of hope—like birdsong
in winter.

Emboldened, I, Margaret Magpie Gabbard, grab
hold of Duby's hand in front of all my kin.

His hand feels so right . . . in mine.

One by one, folks slowly follow suit until we form
a circle—a never-ending chain—not of Goblins or of
sorrows, but of hope.

We circle the giant stone while saying our blessings:

> *God bless you.*
> *God bless me.*
> *God bless this moon that we'll set free.*

And Milo plays his soft sweet music while Talker
sings along.

And it's beautiful. And it's all on key.

We circle three times in one direction.

We circle three times in the other.

With the power coursing through us—the circle,
the blessing and Milo's music—we grab hold of the
giant stone. As one, we lift it up and over on its edge.

And there's the moon's beautiful glowing face looking up at us from a deep hole in the ground. There
ain't no branches—no writhing vines—holding her
back now.

Milo offers the moon his hand.

Milo helps her out of the ground.

And then, Milo, Talker and the moon walk off.

One moment, they're here.

The next, they're lighting up the sky.

Chapter Forty-five
A Beginning

I now got a dull sweet ache inside me. Up here, we call that ache the monthlies. For the first time in my life I've got the monthlies. They came on early this morning—only hours after freeing the moon. When I told Big Mama I had them, she said, "Magpie, you've passed through the gate. You're a woman now."

Well, that was one long gate.

Big Mama says each time I get the monthlies, I'll get special sparkles. Big Mama wants me to use my first batch this morning for a clarifying face-bath. Big Mama wants my face smooth as a peach so I can draw on Duby. Last night, after Milo, Talker and the moon had gone—lighting up the sky like it was on fire—Big Mama saw Duby grab up my hand once more. She heard him say to me, "Magpie Gabbard, I like you. And I like your family."

Oh, I held his hand so tight.

I don't need to clarify my skin to draw on Duby.

Big Mama cornered Sissy Sizemore. Them two had a conversation, the upshot being a fall picnic—all Sizemores, Goforths and Gabbards to be invited. Sissy said she'd bring gunpowder biscuits, guaranteed to taste so good, they'll blow your head off.

Big Mama plans on bringing honey cake.

She says, "I know everyone will like it."

Big Mama's off now, boiling up water for my face-bath.

I'm not ready for a face-bath. I've got other plans. Grabbing the flask, which still has some Green Water in it, I climb out my window. I hurry on over to Grandpa's bee gum. I hold out the key to Wild Bill's heart and call to the boar. He comes trotting out from his nest in the nearby brush.

Key in hand, I head on down the mountain with Wild Bill trotting beside me. A fresh breeze blows through my hair. It's the first breeze I've felt in two weeks. It causes leaves to shower over Wild Bill and me. We kick up our heels. Lord, it feels good to have the moon back!

By early afternoon, we're at Tam's well.

"Tam! I brought you your hog!" I shout.

Tam bobs to the surface.

He's a sorry sight—all scratched and covered in burrs.

Tam and Wild Bill butt heads.

I say to Tam, "How about a comb-through?"

He says, "Pilgrim, I never thought you'd ask."

I never thought I would either. I pull that old head out of the well and set him in my lap. I dip Granny's comb in Green Water and I work through Tam's burrs and tangles while he sighs in contentment. I pat Green Water on Tam's face to clear up his scratches and to ease the hurt of them boils. Them boils dry up and then, they disappear.

I don't believe it.

When I'm all done, Tam sighs and says, "Do I look like a proper head?"

"Take a peek." I hold him over the well water so's he can see his amazing reflection. He says, "I'm one dapper Head. Pilgrim, your kindness has restored me. I can go home."

He asks me to carry him over to the spot off the Cob Hollow Path where Goblins had buried his gray mare, Bess. Before I do, I offer Tam the key to Wild

Bill's heart. He says, "It's yours now, Pilgrim—to do as you wish.

"Treat the old boar kindly," Tam says.

I place Tam on top of his mare's burial spot.

"Now back away," he says.

Soon as I do, he cries out, "Bess, the curse is broken. I'm a free man! It's on to England!" And that gray mare rears out of the Cob Hollow muck. Her flowing mane wraps itself around Tam, forming a basket of hair for him to nestle in.

"Farewell, Pilgrim!" Tam cries.

Bess catapults herself into the blue October sky. As she does, I see a chain of Goblins attached to her tail. She pulls a long chain of Goblins out of the dark Cob Hollow muck and up into the sunlight. They'll never survive that sunlight.

"Farewell, Goblins!" I scream as they disappear into the bright blue sky.

And then, I do what I suppose is the kindest thing for Wild Bill. Something a Pilgrim might do. I offer him the key to his heart.

Wild Bill swallows it.

But he don't take off for England the way them others did. I reckon this old boar loves Kentucky as much as I do, for he follows me back up Gabbard

Mountain. At my grandpa's bee gum, Wild Bill veers off—disappearing into nearby brush. No doubt, he'll be hanging around there, waiting for me to rob the bee gum.

No doubt, I'll be ready for him.